A

CASTLE

FOR SALE

A MONSTROUS MERRY CHRISTMAS TALE

Louise Dando-Collins

A CASTLE FOR SALE
A Monstrous Merry Christmas Tale

First published in 2015
Louise Dando-Collins, The Nunnery, Beaconsfield.

ISBN 13 – 978-1530517954
       10 - 1530517958

I would like to pay tribute to my husband,
Stephen Dando-Collins, for his inspiration.
He has made a great contribution to the
world of literature through his versatile mind,
and total dedication.

My special thanks to Robyn Jones at 1842.

May my humble work of merry fiction –
bring smiles to all those who need them.

Louise Dando-Collins

"Imagination is the only weapon in the war against reality"

-   Lewis Carroll, *Alice in Wonderland.*

CHAPTER 1

"There it is," yelled Robert Campbell from the back seat of Angus McBain's red Range Rover. "There!" He pointed over the shoulder of his father who sat in the front seat. "Look, Katie," the ten year-old said excitedly to his seven year old sister with a nudge in the ribs. She'd been sitting slumped, head to one side, asleep. "Look, up there on the cliff. Wow... it's ancient! Hey Dad, this one's real cool!"

Katie woke with a start wondering what the fuss was about. She rubbed her eyes. "Where? Where is it, Robert?" she asked, sliding forward on the bouncy leather seat to try and see the very last castle for the day, her eyes scanning the horizon.

"Duck down, stupid. It's up on the hillside above us now."

Sure enough, there was the turreted Castle Airde atop its own rocky headland, overlooking Lake Beiste, as if it were a great monster fast asleep and waiting for someone to wake it. The family were in the remote Scottish Highlands now, where the wind blew the heather flat, and the deer roamed free. This great castle stood glowing golden in the late afternoon sunlight, and looked as if it had jumped straight out of a story book.

"Robert! How many times have I told you not to use that 'stupid' word?" said Jean Campbell, the children's mother, who sat cradling tiny two year-old Dorothea, affectionately known as Dottie. There was a tired, irritable tone to the voice of the usually good-natured woman. It had been a long, fruitless week, trying to find the perfect Scottish castle.

"Sorry mum," the boy said quickly, hoping to forestall a full-blown lecture.

Duncan Campbell the children's father spoke out. "It er, looks a bit run down, Mr MacBain he said worriedly to the real estate man, as he too strained to view the castle, way up on the cliff top.

"Och no, Mr Campbell, sir, I've saved the best till last," said Angus, who now turned the steering wheel hard left to drive the vehicle on toward a steep climb. Up the narrow, private road they went onto the castle grounds, and through a series of dark tunnels to the promontory where the castle had been built, and had stood for centuries. "I'm sure this castle is just what you're looking for!" The kindly MacBain had laboured for seven days in bleak weather, treacherous mountain terrain, and the hazardous, narrow roadways which criss-crossed the Highlands, to show the Campbell family from Australia every conceivable style of castle. Castle Airde was the last one on offer.

Duncan Campbell had long held a dream. He had wanted to own a Scottish castle just like his great-great-grandfather had done in the 18th Century. Preferably a castle with a ghost, young Robert had said.

Born in Dundee, which sat on the River Tay on the east coast of Scotland, Duncan had emigrated with his family to Sydney Australia when he was just a boy. But he had vowed to return, and having sold his computer software business, and now with money in the bank, he was emigrating back to Scotland with his own little family to fulfil his dream.

"Does the road go all the way up, Mr MacBain?" asked Robert.

"Aye, laddie, it does. Indeed it does. But hang on tight, it's a mighty hard climb, even for this big lug of a motor. This road was cut out of solid rock you know, and there was a mighty forest protecting it. Just like the ones you've read about in Robin Hood."

"Nottingham Forest?"

"Aye. That's the one, laddie. And there's some say that the famous Robin Hood was none other than Scotland's William

Wallace himself! A giant of a man. A great warrior, a patriot; a renegade, who bravely fought until his dying breath for Scotland's independence."

Duncan Campbell shared a wry smile with his wife Jean.

"William Wallace's name is sacred throughout Scotland, even today. He's a legend. And..." MacBain added, conspiratorially, in a hushed fashion, "the great man is said to have rested here at Airde, in this very castle when he was fleeing King Edward's troops after the battle of Falkirk, way back in 1298."

Young Robert glanced quickly over at Katie with an excited look on his face. "Does the castle have any ghosts, Mr MacBain?"

MacBain gave the boy a winsome smile.

Jean spoke out. "I warned you Robert, there will be no scary ghost stories," she scolded, on seeing Katie's worried look.

McBain took up the conversation again. "And you'll find, Mr Campbell, sir, that the defenders cleverly blocked off pathways to the top, in not one, but in fourteen different places to trick the invading armies that wanted to plunder the castle, and take the jewels of Scotland. There are tunnels running throughout the whole cliff – like a maze."

"Wow! Bet they're full of ghosts," said Robert, his eyes alight, as he darted a glance over at Katie's look of concern, as little Dottie slept on.

"Is it much further?" asked Jean, weary after their many days of searching.

"Just a wee bit further," said MacBain, as he traversed the long and winding dark tunnels marked with arrows pointing up toward the castle, and down toward the exit, so as not to get lost going either way.

"I can see a light at the end of the tunnel Mr MacBain. See it Katie?"

"Yes," she answered, rubbing her tired eyes.

"Nearly there," said MacBain.

The dot of light grew bigger and bigger, until the blue/grey sky of the fading daylight came into view. Until, with the roar of the engine, the great vehicle emerged from the endlessly long, narrow, snake-like tunnel. The family from Australia could only be described as gobsmacked, when they saw the majestic Castle Airde spread out in front of them at the summit.

"What a sight!" Duncan exclaimed.

"Oh, my Goodness," said Jean, a smile breaking out on her lovely face.

"A fairy tale castle..." said young Katie, dreamily.

"WOW! This is sure to have ghosts!" said Robert.

The vision of this ancient structure – a mighty walled citadel on the crest of Airde Mountain, with snow-capped peaks in the distance every which way they looked, and with beautiful Lake Airde eight hundred feet below almost encircling them, had taken them all by surprise.

"And look! It has its own drawbridge!" Robert couldn't believe his luck.

"Well now, what d'you think, Mrs Campbell, Mr Campbell?" said MacBain with a great grin on his face, as he glided the vehicle around the circular driveway to park at the entrance.

With a quick glance over at his precious wife before he made any comment, Duncan could see Jean was impressed, but he was cautious with his answer. "Er, are you sure this is in our price range, Mr MacBain?"

"'Tis indeed. It is indeed," answered MacBain pulling on the handbrake.

Robert and Katie were quickly out and running toward the drawbridge which stood over a twenty foot deep moat, and the pair were soon into a fierce and fanciful sword fight.

"Be careful children," cried Jean, handing the now wide awake Dottie to Duncan, then running with the children's new duffle coats to keep them warm. "Put on your coats - or you brave knights of old - will be in bed with a cold," she said, smiling to herself, thinking how clever she was.

"Oh, Mum!" they said in unison, stopping their fight to give her a scowl.

The family walked together in a group and listened as MacBain explained a few things about the castle. "Sadly, a few of the outbuildings are in ruin, but to my mind, that only adds to the romance of the place," he said with a twinkle in his mischievous eyes. "But, considering that this castle dates back to 1260 or thereabouts, it's in remarkably good condition."

"That's really old," said Katie.

"And it's a deceased estate you see, Mr Campbell, sir. Lord Hamish who owned it last was a Campbell - he was Lord Hamish McPorridge Campbell, and it would be a great thing if another Campbell were to buy it. I er, don't suppose you're related?"

"Not that I know of..." said Duncan.

"Of course there's a title that goes with the property," MacBain was quick to add.

"A title?" Duncan queried suspiciously, thinking it would likely cost him money.

"Aye. The title of 'Lord of The Manor of Airde.' Did I not tell you that before?"

"Lord of The Manor? Did you hear that, Jean?" He glanced at Robert and Katie to see if they were impressed.

"Yes, Your Lordship. So let's hurry in then, before it gets any darker." MacBain unlocked the mighty old door, which opened with a croaking dry creek. "And of course, it comes fully furnished." MacBain looked over at Jean, cleverly knowing this would please most women, and he could tell that she was very impressed. "Yes, just the way the last owner left it. Full of antiques, it is!"

"But tell us about the ghosts, Mr MacBain..."

"Robert!"

"Boys will be boys," MacBain chortled. Then he gave Robert a sly wink.

Chapter 2

A loud crack on wood was heard throughout the grand entrance hall, and it made Jean Campbell gasp in fright. She was about to climb the mahogany staircase up to the bedrooms with clean linen in her arms, and her mind had been focussed on the task at hand. She felt a tad nervous about opening the door, as her husband Duncan was in the village on business, and she was alone with the children. She set the bedding down on a nearby table, while the knock on the great front door was repeated again, and again.

Sliding back the iron bolt, and tugging with all her might, she opened the heavy door with a rusty screech, and was surprised to find a crumpled-looking little old man on her doorstep. Only as tall as Katie, the man looked like a Pixie, dressed as he was in long boots, green breeches, waistcoat and peaked cap. His ruddy complexion was furrowed like the bark of an old elm tree, and his eyes, set widely apart, sloped upwards at the outer corner and pointed to his ears.

"Yeees?" she braved.

Off came the peaked cap, the wide eyes crinkled until they disappeared into the folds of his wrinkled skin, and when he spoke, it was ever so softly, like a sweet child, and Jean had to bend close to hear him.

"Good morning t' you, your Ladyship. I'm the Ghillie, ma'am. Jock Baird's the name," the aged Scotsman said, before bowing respectfully.

"The... Ghillie?"

"Yes, m'lady. I'm here to work for ye, Mrs Campbell."

"Oh, thank you, but I have it all under control now," she smiled warmly at the stranger.

"But I come wi' the castle, m'lady," the little man insisted.

"You do?"

"Aye. I come wi' the castle! When you bought the castle, you bought me as well. It's been written in the castle deed since time immemorial. The eldest member of the Baird family shall serve the Lord of The Manor from his first day, till his last. Aye, since time immemorial. Just the same way the village is expectin' that Mr Campbell will perform his duties, as Laird."

"His duties?"

"Och, aye, m'lady. Being the Laird of Airde is a great responsibility. Did ye not know that?"

"Why, er, no, Mr Baird. I didn't, and neither did my husband," Jean said, perplexed. "I think you'd better come inside and tell me exactly what it is that you do."

#

Sitting at the cosy end of the twenty-two foot long kitchen table, with his back to the flaming log fire in the stone fireplace, which was big enough for eight grown men to stand in, side by side, the Ghillie began to tell his tale. The Campbell children and their mother sat enthralled, listening to this puckish little man explain in almost a whisper, what it meant to be the Ghillie. A plate of delicious Scottish shortbread, and mugs of steaming hot chocolate, there for all.

"I'm the gamekeeper," he began, "but I must admit, being the honest man that I am, that I find it a bit heavy going these days, so I get young Lachlan MacGregor to keep an eye on things for me," he said with a wink to the smiling Katie, who had taken quite a shine to the elfin-like man. And I'm the gatekeeper as well, ye know. But we lost the key to the gate many a long year ago, so we just keep it open nowadays."

Robert and his mother shared a grin.

"And I'm the timekeeper. But I'm sorry t' say, that the Village Hall clock is broken. Been that way for nigh on 100 years now, and no one seems able to fix it!" He shook his head in bewilderment. "And I'm also the lawn keeper."

"But there's no lawn to keep?" asked Jean, good-naturedly.

"Och, aye, there's a grand lawn on the Village Green, but my bad back has prevented me from keepin' the lawn shorn these days, so I've taken t' borrowin' auld Jessie McFarlane's prize sheep, Jessi-Belle, and she keeps it shorn for me. Now, what else is there that I'm called upon to do?" He closed his eyes and thought hard about his duties, and while he did, the close-knit family shared a cheeky little secret smile between them, for they thought Jock Baird, the Ghillie, an eccentric, quaint little man, but they didn't want to offend him.

"I do odd jobs, Mrs Campbell. Any wee job that's needin' done around the place. Anythin' at all that ye need doin'."

"Oh, well, that will be very handy, thank you, Mr Baird."

"Except that I suffer from vertigo." He looked over at the children's bewildered looks. "That means that I canna stand heights, ye know. So I canna climb ladders. And I canna swim. And, what wi' my arthritis, and my bad back, I'm prevented from lifting anything. And if I bend down, I get dizzy, ye know." He nodded his head. "But there's always young Lachlan to lend a hand. And o'course my eyesight is failin' me, and I could never depend on my hearin'." He looked into Jean's eyes. "Apart from that yer Ladyship, I'm yours t' command."

Jean Campbell had to bite her lip to prevent herself from laughing out loud. She too, was quite taken with the Ghillie, but knew he would be of no practical use to the family. But anyone

12

that brought a smile to her face was welcome in the Campbell home.

"How much are we expected to pay you, Mr Baird?"

The Ghillie is paid a sovereign a year," Mrs Campbell. In today's money, that's a Scottish pound. Now then," he said, as he rose to leave, "has anyone told you about The Chapel?"

"Well no... but we haven't had time to explore everything yet."

"Well, that would be a waste of yer good time anyway, because I'm the one wi' the key." He grinned at Robert, before reaching down into the leather pouch at his hip to withdraw a foot-long key, to the surprise of everyone, then he swivelled from the long kitchen bench and stood. "Come wi' me and I'll show ye." And off he moved, as Robert, Katie, and little Dottie scampered after him in the direction of the long, dark, west wing of the castle.

#

Ancient, long-dead warriors of the Campbell clan looked down at them from paintings hung on the inner walls of the castle. The haunting eyes of the deceased ancestors painted in the portraits, seemed to follow them as they walked, and Katie was heard to say, 'It's scary down here,' as it grew darker, with every step they took.

Again, as if by magic, the Ghillie reached down into his satchel, and this time pulled out a powerful torch to light their way. Eventually, they came to a great oak door, not unlike the castle's main front door, and the Ghillie unlocked it with the foot-long key. A moan, a groan, and a long, lazy creak emanated from its un-oiled hinges, to reveal a heavenly white chapel. A cosy, beautifully pristine chamber, with coloured glass windows behind the altar, which glowed with the shining sun from the morning sky.

"It is said," the Ghillie began, "that The Guardian himself came here to contemplate his destiny."

13

"The Guardian?" queried Robert.

"Aye, laddie. Sir William Wallace – The Guardian of Scotland. He kindled the spirit of independence in Scotland that was never extinguished. His love for this bonnie land can still be felt in this place. He was a braw patriot, and a braw, brave man."

Little Dottie, who had been very well behaved, clinging to her mother's hand, suddenly cried out, "Big Man!" and pointed through the tiny chapel to the altar at the far end, where only a red velvet cloth lay draped over a huge flat slab of rock. This rock supported a magnificent pair of gold candelabras, each holding fifty unlit candles. And behind it, sat a grand chair, like a King's throne, with great furs draped over it.

"Aye, ye bonny wee lassie," the Ghillie smiled. "He was indeed a big man. A giant of a man at that. Over seven feet tall, they say."

Jean, Robert and Katie Campbell all looked at little Dottie simultaneously. Amazed by her outburst, and wondered what on earth made her say such a thing out of the blue.

"Big Man's chair," she said, with a smile that stretched from ear to ear, and she pointed again in the direction of the chair.

"Aye, lass. That stone chair has always been known as The Guardian's Throne, for William Wallace himself would sit there.

"Oh, how romantic," sighed Jean.

"It's a grand place for ye to come and melt away a few of your worries, m'lady. A visit here will rejuvenate you. There's no doubt about that!" He turned and began to walk solemnly away. Silently, he held open the door for them all to pass through, and they turned and watched him as he closed it with reverence.

What he did not see, was little Dottie standing behind her mother's back, smiling, and waving back down through the chapel, as if she were saying goodbye to an old friend.

14

"I won't lock the door, m'lady, but I'll leave the key with you. Look after it though, for it locks, and unlocks most of the doors in the castle."

"Thank you, Mr Baird. I'll keep it on the hook by the fireplace in the kitchen."

"I'll return to explain the duties of Laird of Airde to his Lordship, Mr Campbell, another day," he said to Jean, shaking her hand, before she returned with Dottie to the kitchen, while Robert and Katie walked the Ghillie back to the castle's grand front door.

Now Robert took the opportunity to ask the question which was uppermost in his mind. "Are there any ghosts in our castle, Mr Baird?"

"Ghosts?" said Jock. "Och aye laddie, I'm sure ye know that all castles are said to be haunted." He smiled.

"There are ghosts?" Robert glanced round at Katie with a grin. "Do you hear that, Katie. We've got ghosts!"

"Stop it Robert, you know I'm frightened of ghosts."

"Och, there's no need to be frightened, lassie," said the little old man, patting Katie's head. "There's only the one ghost. But a very special ghost indeed. A very nice ghost."

"Tell me about it, Mr Baird," said Robert excitedly.

"I hav'na got the time to tell ye any stories now, laddie, but I promise to tell ye all, the next time I come to the castle." He smiled a wry smile at Robert with an added wink, turned, put his peaked cap back on his head, and hobbled down the twelve front steps.

Robert stood stunned thinking about what the Ghillie had told him. For here he was, living in a fantastic medieval castle, with its very own ghost.

"Race you back to the kitchen, Katie?" he blurted, and dashed off to tell his mother.

"Wait! Wait for me Robert. Don't leave me here by myself. Wait!" Katie wailed, and took off after her brother as fast as her legs could carry her, though knowing she could never catch him. Robert was a long-distance, fast runner. She was a dancer. But it didn't stop her from trying to compete - at everything.

#

The following week, Duncan Campbell sat down with the Ghillie to learn what his duties as Laird of Airde would be. The cosy fireside end of the kitchen table, which dominated the stone-floored kitchen, had become the family meeting place.

"The first thing I'll have to arrange for y' m'lord, Mr Campbell, sir, is to swear the oath of Justice of the Peace, so that ye can perform your list of duties as Laird of Airde and local magistrate."

"Local Magistrate, eh?" Duncan smiled proudly. "And tell me Ghillie, just what are these duties?"

"Well now. I've made a list so that I did'na forget anythin'," and he reached for a tattered piece of paper in his breast pocket, then read it out. "Ye'll have to sign all the official documents of the village, and officiate at all the weddings – sign as principal witness, y' understand. And give a wee present to the beautiful bride."

"Okay. Sounds like a bit of fun. Anything else?"

"Ye'll be the Chief Judge of the district's Highland Dancing Competition, y' ken."

"That means 'you know,' dad," Katie chimed in authoritatively.

"Yes, thank you, Katherine," said her father.

"And it'll be your job to sign all the fishing licences for the fishermen that fish on Loch Beiste. Aye, an ye'll have to attend all of the Christenings, and provide for a glass o' whisky for every man in attendance. And there's always a good turnout for that." He looked up from his notes to make sure that Duncan understood his

16

duties so far, then returned his eyes to the list in front of him. "And should there be a death, and God forbid there should," he said, shaking his head mournfully, "and the deceased is a pauper, then it's the Laird's duty to pay for the funeral."

"Really?" Duncan frowned. "Er, are there many paupers in Airde?"

"Och, there's no need t' worry, m'lord," the Ghillie said, reassuringly, "the last person that died aroond here was a hundred years ago. And there's only a few of us in the village that's over sixty-five years of age. We prefer to live a long time in Airde," which was followed by the little grin that made his eyes disappear into the creases of his wrinkled face. "Nobody likes the undertaker, so we dinna want t' give him any business."

"Well that's good to hear! So, Ghillie, that's pretty well covered everything – births, deaths, and marriages. Is there anything else I should know?"

"Well of course ye'll have t' buy the first salmon caught each season. At a cost of one golden guinea – and present the fish to the local minister of the church."

Duncan glanced over at Jean and raised his eyebrows. "Quaint," he commented. "Is that the extent of my duties then Ghillie?"

"Well o' course, ye'll be the Chairman of the Progress Association. But there's little work to be done aboot that, for there's little in the way of progress in Airde these days. Major Fordyce makes sure of that – he's the enemy of progress aroond these parts."

"Who's Major Fordyce?" young Robert dared to ask.

"Old Bulldog, I call him. An Englishman. He has almost total control of the village. His property lies on either side of the entrance road. He knows everything that happens, and knows whoever comes and goes. He came to the village of Airde for the peace and quiet, and Lord help anyone who disturbs it!"

Duncan was beginning to wonder what would happen to his own peace and quiet. If what the Ghillie said was true, once he commenced his duties, he wouldn't have a minute to himself, let alone have time to earn a living.

"Surely the Major has a friendly side, Mr Baird?" said Jean demurely.

"I doubt ye'll get to see the Major's friendly side, m'lady. I doubt that anybody's ever seen it. We decided long ago that the man doesna' have a friendly side. And I should warn you, that he was far happier with an absentee landlord of Airde Castle. Much happier before ye came here, that is. I wouldn't be a bit surprised if you had a visit from him any day now. He'll be wantin' to lay down the law according t' Fordyce. And he'll bring that smelly slaverin' dog Magnus with him, to be sure. A more unpleasant animal I've never had the misfortune to meet."

"What sort of dog is he, Mr Baird?" Robert asked.

"An ugly British bulldog that's he's trained like a canine commando, laddie."

The Campbell family looked from one to the other, sharing thoughts of concern about this Major Fordyce and his unfriendly dog. And, Duncan Campbell in particular, had a most disconsolate frown etched on his face. He was thinking about all the time-consuming duties he had to perform, which had the possibility of making a big hole in his money pocket. This worried look did not go undetected by his youngest daughter. Little two-year-old Dottie, a very likeable, bright child, who leaned her head to one side, looked up into her Daddy's face, and made an astute, considered comment, 'Daddy look sad, Mummy!' But it sounded more like 'thad' because little Dottie, couldn't quite master all of her words yet.

Chapter 3

The Ghillie's prediction proved true, when first thing next morning, promptly at nine, the Campbells received their first visit from Major Fordyce, and his ugly dog Magnus.

From his cute little cottage, at the fork of the village road, and the narrow road which wound high up to the castle, Jock Baird, the Ghillie, had seen Major Fordyce drive by and turn off, heading toward Castle Airde, and had telephoned a warning to the Campbells. So when a dark green Land Rover drew up at the castle drawbridge, the whole Campbell family peeked through the windows of The Grand Hall to watch, and spy on him.

The heavy vehicle's engine stopped. The driver's side door slowly opened. A portly man of sixty years emerged, with an angry expression, and an enormous, curled moustache. He wore a thick, checked, Harris Tweed jacket and jodhpurs, with matching deer-stalker cap, scarf and waistcoat, with black Wellington boots which came up to his knees. And he carried a walking-stick with an ivory-topped handle, which was in the shape of a gun. He was escorted by his wide, short-legged, over-fed black dog, which he had to physically help out of the Land Rover because of its bulk. Then, with the dog at his side, he marched up to the castle entrance and rapped impatiently on the door-knocker.

Jean Campbell moved to answer the door, but Duncan held her back.

"Just a minute, Jean. I'll see to Major Fordyce. This relationship must get off to a good start," he announced, then his face broke out into a mischievous smile, adding, "So we'll let the man wait a while, shall we?"

"Oh, Duncan!" Jean scolded. "Let's not upset him. We musn't be as difficult as he is! That's certainly not the way to start a good relationship."

"If the grumpy old man wants to be difficult, then let him. I am the master of this household Jean Campbell, and the new Lord of the Manor. AND, I might add, The Laird of Airde! He should be made to respect that from the very beginning."

"As you wish," said Jean, standing back, thinking to herself that the new 'Lord of the Manor' title had gone to her husband's head, just a little. With luck, she hoped, once the novelty wore off, he might return to his normal delightful self.

The thunderous sound of three more, sharp angry raps filled the castle foyer before the children saw their father open the door to the Major, and, true to form, the great oak door gave out its familiar long, drawn-out rusty squeak. No matter how much oil had been applied to the hinges, it defiantly continued to make this agonising rusty squeal.

"Good morning," said Duncan with a smile to the stranger. "How may I help you?"

"Fordyce is my name." The major looked the Lord of the Manor - The Lair of Airde, up and down disapprovingly. "Major Fordyce. Ex-army Major, I'll have you know."

"Yes, what can I do for you, Mr Fordyce?"

"Major Fordyce, if you please," he corrected sourly. "Surely the Ghillie has told you who I am." His manner was pompous in the extreme.

"Ah, yes, Major Fordyce. Do come in. You're more than welcome. But please, could you leave the dog outside?"

At this, the dog looked up at Duncan and growled a low, menacing growl.

"I beg your pardon," Fordyce spluttered. "I'll have you know that Magnus goes everywhere with me."

"That may be so, Major Fordyce, but our family does not permit dogs in the house."

"Humph! Well, in that case I'll say what I have to say right here, if I'm not permitted to have my dog Magnus accompany me inside."

"As you wish."

"Humph!" He cleared his throat. "Humph!" he repeated. "Now then, Campbell," he began.

"Duncan's the name," said Duncan with a warm smile, holding out his hand to shake the Major's leather-gloved hand.

Fordyce ignored Duncan's outstretched hand of friendship. "You'll be 'Campbell' to me, my man," he declared, shaking his walking-stick angrily at Duncan. "'Campbell.' Do you hear?"

"Yes, I do hear you." Duncan glared at the man, "I am not deaf, Major Fordyce."

"Humph! Don't be a smart aleck with me, m'lad. I came here to Airde Village for peace and quiet, and a stress-free life. Just don't you go doing anything to this place that will threaten that peace and quiet! I don't want Airde overrun with tourists or foreign business executives. Do you hear me, Campbell? I will not have some rich young whipper-snapper foreigner, upsetting my apple-cart!"

"Well, Major Fordyce, I'm neither rich, nor a foreigner – I was born in Dundee, though I have lived for much of my life in Australia, which is an independent and very pleasant nation. If it's peace you want, I suggest that you return to your home and live in peace, and allow me to do the same. Good morning to you, Major."

And with that, Duncan pushed closed the door on the frosty old Major, and from inside, the Campbell family could hear the grumpy man 'Humph' and mumble angrily to himself all the way back to the Land Rover. While the children in the castle giggled to themselves, they watched Fordyce struggle to lift, and thrust his ugly dog Magnus back into the vehicle. It departed with a screech on the gravel, and a swirl of dust.

#

Several days later, Castle Airde had another visitor. A Mrs Euphemia MacGivacuddle came aknocking. And the first thing she did when greeted at the door by Jean Campbell was – hiccup!

"Och, ah'm so verra verra sorry, Mrs Campbell, your ladyship. Ah only do it when ah'm nervous. Hic! Och, there I go again! I'm Euphemia MacGivacuddle. The Ghillie said I should be seein' you. Hic!"

"There's no need to be nervous. Come on in, Mrs Mac... Givacuddle is it?"

"Aye. Hic! It is. But just call me Effie."

"Oh, I wouldn't dream of it. Euphemia is such a lovely name. Do come in. The Ghillie told us that we've inherited you and your services. I'm certainly pleased to have you - I'm lost in this big house. I can't find anything. And nothing seems to work as it should."

"Thank you, Mrs Campbell, m'lady, Hic!" said Effie, who, it turned out, had been the previous owner's domestic servant, or 'charlady' as they were called in Scotland. "Ah would've come last week, but ah was feelin' a wee bit poorly. Hic!"

Jean led her through to the warm kitchen where, unbeknownst to Jean, Effie had spent most of her working hours - with the previous owner away most of the time - sitting by the fire, fast asleep. For, as the Campbells would soon find out, Euphemia MacGivacuddle had a habit of putting whisky in her morning's porridge, whisky in her soup at lunch time, and whisky in her stew at dinner. And, if the chance presented itself, the rosy-cheeked Effie would sip a glass of the whisky at any time at all. Jean would come to describe her, as being reliably – unreliable!

But that very first week, poor Effie got such a fright at the castle under the employ of her new employers, that she nearly swore off the whisky for life. And it was all because of little Dottie.

Since moving into the castle, the tiny two-year-old had taken to disappearing, sometimes for an hour at a time. The little mite was not at all afraid to roam the castle by herself. It was Robert who was sent to look for her each time, for Katie was too afraid of the dark hallways to search by herself.

"Dottie? Dottie? Where are you, you dottie little girl," shouted Robert, heading down the east wing where there was a grand fireplace Dottie used as a cubby house. "How many times has mum told you not to wander off and disappear?"

"And how many times have I told you not to call her Dottie," called his mother from the kitchen. Her name is Dorothea. Please use it!" Jean said with annoyance, though she had been quite happily making apple pies in the kitchen with Effie, until then.

"Sorry mum," Robert yelled back, adding, "Dorothea's such a silly name," he said under his breath, as he headed off down the corridor to search. "Sounds like something that grows in the garden."

"Ah'll just put these tasty wee pies in the oven for you, m'lady and give the young lad a hand to look for the bairn," said the well-meaning Effie, dusting off her hands before pulling open the Aga's heavy door. Effie slid in her tray of apple pies, took off her flour-stained apron, washed her hands, then joined the search for the baby of the family.

"Thank you, Euphemia. She's quite a handful now that she's taken to wandering." Shaking her head, Jean took up a rolling pin, thumped it on the pastry and continued cooking.

#

Effie headed straight down to the west wing, which was still morbidly dim, regardless of the fact that Duncan had connected a new light fitting half way down the corridor. But this suited Effie just fine, this was a great hiding place. For here, outside the chapel was a wide ledge under a window, where she could sit and sip her beloved whisky till her flask was empty.

"Dorothea, Dorothea," she cried out in her Scottish brogue, until she thought she was out of earshot, then, she just kept on walking till she came to the chapel. There, she sat on the ledge, put her feet up, pulled out her whisky flask and drank it dry, then promptly fell asleep.

It wasn't until thirty minutes had passed that she woke with a start, rubbed her eyes, and remembered what she was meant to be doing. She shook her head as if to clear it, opened the door of the chapel, and lo and behold, the sight before her eyes made her fall to the floor. For there was little Dottie - flying in mid-air. Ten feet off the ground, arms out-stretched, with the biggest grin on her pretty little face, giggling and humming to herself as if she were dancing with an invisible giant.

Effie staggered away from the chapel. "Och, dearie, dearie me, ah've taken to imagining things! Hic! It must be the whisky, it must be the whisky," she groaned in disbelief, holding her head. She didn't dare tell anyone what she had seen. Who would believe her?

Chapter 4

A very grave matter indeed raised its head within the first few weeks at the castle. When Duncan Campbell opened his mail at the Post Office one morning, he found a quote to fix the castle plumbing that ran into thousands of dollars.

"This can't be right, Jean," said Duncan as he settled down at the kitchen table to have a chat and a cup of tea with Jean, having just returned home after taking Robert and Katie to the village school.

Dottie, too young to attend school, sat with her parents drawing, and looked up anxiously when she heard the tone of her father's voice. Deciding that he was unhappy again, she resumed her sketch of a Scottish Thistle, the flower of Scotland, which looked more like a chubby pygmy with a bad haircut.

"Alistair Hamilton is asking for an astronomical sum of money to fix our plumbing." said Duncan, handing Jean the hand-written quote. When she examined it, her jaw dropped, and her mouth hung open at the amount of money it would take to fix the rusty pipes.

It was now the cold month of November, Christmas was drawing near, and in Scotland's Highlands, before the beautiful snow begins to fall each winter, the rain comes down in buckets; and buckets is what the family were forced to collect it in - from the ceiling of every room of the castle - because the roof leaked all over the place.

It drizzled in through gaps in window ledges. It dripped down from cracks in ceilings, to sometimes play a tune on a spoon in a bowl on the kitchen table. There were puddles in the parlour, and it trickled down the staircase like an inside waterfall. And yet... there was none where it was needed - in the kitchen or the bathroom.

"Oh dear," said Jean, "It's such a nuisance when I turn on the tap and no water comes out. Angus MacBain was extremely remiss not to warn us that the pipes were all rusty. Now we'll have to pump our water from the well in the courtyard."

"I can't have you doing that my dear, and certainly not in this weather! There was a lot MacBain conveniently 'forgot' to tell us. I thought that buying this castle was all going to be a bit of fun. But I'm way behind in my work because of all these duties I have as Laird of Airde."

"But I do so love the place, Duncan."

"I love it too, Jean. It was my dream, remember? But the bills are piling up!"

"The children are doing so well here, too," Jean added quickly, trying to remind him how happy they all were. "Perhaps there's something I can do to make things easier?"

Duncan looked across the table at his wife and saw a look of concern on her pretty face. "It's not for you to worry yourself over, my dear. You have enough to worry about with the children to look after, and all the things you have to do, to make a comfortable home for us here."

Jean smiled sweetly at her husband. She knew that each one of the family had made sacrifices to allow Duncan to have his long-held dream come true. But being a very practical woman, she would give the matter of their finances some thought.

It was plain for anyone to see, how much Duncan loved to dress up in his great red cloak and gold chain, to perform his ceremonial duties as Laird of Airde. At the first village wedding he'd attended, the groom had shaken his hand so vigorously, that Duncan's hat had fallen off, and his great gold chain had rattled. Then there was the beautiful young bride with Highland heather in

26

her hair, who had kissed Duncan's cheek as if he were Father Christmas. Jean had noted that Duncan blushed with pride. And when Duncan had attended the first Christening, at the quaint old Kirk of Airde, the village church, the people had given him a rousing three cheers. 'Hip Hip Hooray!'

Jean smiled to herself as she thought about how magnificent Duncan looked in his full regalia; his red-velvet cloak and wide-brimmed hat, resplendent with pheasant feathers; and how, with a grand sweep of that hat, he would bow to her, every time he headed off to do his duties. She reached out across the table to him and touched his hand lovingly, giving him one of her best smiles.

It was just then, as the three sat quietly in the kitchen contemplating what they should do, that they heard a snap, a crackle, and a pop overhead, coming from the ceiling light. The three looked up to see dangerous sparks of electricity shooting out from the light fitting. Then there was a whizz, and a fizz, followed by a big bang, then a blackout.

Dottie giggled. But Duncan, with his mind on money-matters, couldn't see the funny side of things, and his worst angry word slipped out. Jean had to remind him that he'd been using it a lot of late.

"Now we'll have to get the electrician as well as the plumber! Where's the torch, Jean?" he blustered.

And Jean, flustered, said, "I er, oh, just a minute Duncan. I'll light this candle and have a look in the scullery," that was the name given to the pantry in Scotland. And she quickly traipsed off to find a torch, as Duncan yelled out to bring the telephone book too.

#

Phoning the village's only electrician at home, Duncan was told by Felicity Ferguson, the electrician's mother, that her son Frank was away mountaineering on Ben Nevis, and that Duncan would have to call an electrician in Inverness. It took five telephone calls to different technicians, explaining how urgent it was that Duncan resume his computer work, before Duncan could find some help. Thomas 'Noddie' Tremble would drive all the way from Dundee to help, only to deliver more bad news.

"It'll cost you a pretty penny, Mr Campbell, Laird, sir," 'Noddie' Tremble said, with a vigorous nodding of his head. "Aye, a pretty penny. The whole castle will have t' be re-wired!"

#

"Thank goodness for the Aga," said Jean to the children, who were happily munching griddle scones with raspberry jam and cream that Effie had made for them, as an after school treat. The Aga oven cooked with wood, and didn't need electricity. "And I was reading that book you left for me, Euphemia," she said to Effie, her reliably unreliable domestic helper.

"And what book was that, m'lady?"

"Why, the book about Bed and Breakfast houses throughout Scotland. It's a grand idea! We have so many rooms here, with a bed and furniture in every one. It's an ideal way to make extra money to help with the family's finances. And you would be such a help to me if I decided to take it on."

Effie's eyebrows shot skyward, her face took on a puzzled look, she raised her shoulders and shrugged, then shook her head in bewilderment. "But ah did'na leave any book for you, m'lady."

"You didn't?" said Jean, looking from Effie to the children in turn.

"Not me," said Katie.

28

"Nor me," said Robert. I only like books about monsters. And ghosts. WHOOOOO!" He was of course trying to scare his sisters, but they ignored him.

"That reminds me, when is the Ghillie coming back? I want to talk to him about our ghost."

Jean's mind was still on the book that lay on the kitchen table. It had suggested the money-making venture of turning the castle into a home-away-from-home for travellers. Castle Airde could become a Bed and Breakfast house - a small hotel which would provided sleeping quarters, and breakfast for guests, before the travellers went on their way again touring the Highlands. She would talk to Duncan about it. But still puzzled about the book, she asked, "well if you two didn't leave it for me, and Effie didn't – who did?"

"Big Man!" exclaimed Dottie.

"Big Man? What big man?" asked Jean.

"Yeth. My Big Man," declared Dottie, her mouth covered in jam.

"You know, mum, this isn't the first time Dottie's spoken about this 'Big Man.' She talks about him all the time."

"She does?" Jean sat down hard on one of the kitchen benches, which was just like a very long piano stool, while Effie threw another log on the fire. "Well don't tell your father just yet, it will only give him something else to worry about. He wouldn't understand an imaginary friend, he'd probably think it would cost him money. Which reminds me, I'm afraid you'll have to play skittles by lamp-light tonight until we have the electricity repaired."

"Alright, mum," said Robert rising from the table with his plate and cup to place them in the sink, with a passing, cheeky, boyish remark to Effie. "Your 'grizzly' scones were great, Effie, thanks!" And, with that, he grabbed up his little sister from her chair, saying, "You're coming with me, you dottie little girl."

"Robert!" scolded his mother. But he was gone with Dottie in a flash, with Katie running on behind.

He was very interested to know what Dottie meant by 'Big Man.'

"Show me this 'Big Man,' Dottie," he said, as he put her down to walk by herself the remainder of the way down the corridor. She led him down the long walkway of the West Wing in the direction of the chapel, with the eyes of the long-dead ancestors watching them from the portraits above.

#

When they came to the chapel door, little Dottie stood on tip-toe and pulled down the heavy metal latch with two hands, all by herself. The door sprung open. Robert and Katie shared a look of admiration, they were often surprised at how smart their little sister was.

"Big Man," she declared, pointing into the chapel.

The older children gave each other a puzzled look.

"Where's 'Big Man?'" asked Robert, slightly annoyed, because as far as he could see, the chapel was empty.

"On chair!" she replied, in her sweet little girl's voice, before running over to the throne-line Guardian's chair to stand beside it, looking up smiling.

'So,' thought Robert, she wants to play games does she? "And just how big is this 'Big Man?" He walked toward her across the stone floor. "As big as this?" He raised one arm in the air above his head.

Dottie shook her head.

"As big as this?" He jumped up onto a stone chapel pew.

"Don't forget where you are, Robert," chided Katie, who was very proper and respectful about such things.

Dottie shook her head again, smiled, then, facing her older brother and sister, lifted both her arms towards the ceiling. 'Up!' she gestured.

"What? Taller than this?" Robert queried in disbelief, reaching as high as he could in the air.

"Up!" Dottie said aloud.

"Don't be stupid, Dottie Campbell!" Robert jumped down to the ground. "Nobody's that tall. You're only making it up!" he declared, and headed for the door feeling a bit put out, as if he'd been cheated and lost at a game of cards. "Sometimes you really are dottie, Dottie! Come on, Katie, let's go play skittles," and he ran out of the chapel with Katie at his heel.

Dottie didn't follow on. Had her brother and sister stayed, they would have witnessed an eery sight in the afternoon light streaming in through the chapel window. For Dottie was suddenly lifted magically into the air, and, giggling with glee, flittered around the chapel as if flying in an invisible little helicopter.

Chapter 5

As dawn broke in the hills and glens around the village of Airde on this late November morning, the cheeky squirrel, the grouse, the hedgehog, and the tortoise, enjoyed a long early winter sleep, while in ancient icy water meadows, inquisitive otters playfully braved the fast-moving streams, to slide down snow-covered banks, and catch their fish. The deer, the fox, the stoat and the hare, foraged for food in desolate, mountainous frozen terrain. And as the weak late autumn sun peeked around the mist-cloaked hills, delicate white snow-flakes floated gently from the heavens, to present the Campbell children at Castle Airde with their very first experience of snow.

"Look, Katie! Dottie! Look, real snow!" cried Robert excitedly, barging into his sisters' bedroom, and bounding over to their window to pull back the drapes, urging the girls to jump out of bed and share this early morning surprise. It would be the one time Katie did not scold him for entering the girls' bedroom without knocking.

Katie lifted up her little sister to take in the breathtaking sight of gentle snowflakes drifting past the window in the eery magic light of dawn. Everything, as far as the eye could see was coated with icy petals; the lake and the sky had merged into one white mist. Eyes alight at the wonder of it, the three huddled together to make plans to build their very first snowman.

In the main bed-room, the grown-ups were woken from their cosy night's slumber by the haunting sound of a lone piper playing his bagpipes.

"What the devil is that?" Duncan asked, sitting bolt upright in bed at the warming-up squawking and squealing of the unique Scottish wind instrument - the famous bagpipes.

Jean slid out of bed and pulled the curtains back to look down at the castle entrance, to see a young piper in full Highland regalia – kilt, sporran, tartan stockings, jacket and bonnet. "Oh, my goodness, it's a young Scottish piper playing for us, Duncan. But he'll catch his death of cold out there," Jean exclaimed. "Look, it's snowing, and he's standing out there in the snow with bare knees. I think we should invite him in." She hurried to put on a robe. "I'll make extra porridge, and he can join us for breakfast," and she fled to the kitchen to prepare for their guest. She made a full pot of porridge, boiled fresh eggs, poached some kippers, fried tasty sausages, and had mountains of toast ready within minutes.

After stoking up the glowing embers of the kitchen fire with three extra-large logs of wood, Duncan, dressed in fur-lined boots, a thick woollen coat, a knitted scarf, hat and mittens, braved the icy morning, and ventured outside to welcome the piper.

When the piper's melancholy lament concluded, Duncan marched across the bridge toward the tartan-clad piper on the thin white blanket of freshly fallen snow, his footprints marking his way, and held out his hand in greeting to the young man. "Good morning to you, piper. I'm Duncan Campbell, The Laird."

The piper, a handsome young man of twenty-five, tall, and broad shouldered, smiled and shook his hand. "Good morning to you, Laird. I'm Lachlan MacGregor, the Laird of Airde's ceremonial piper."

"Oh, and how much am I supposed to pay you for that?" Duncan asked suspiciously. All the costs associated with being Lord of the Manor were beginning to add up.

"Och, no, you don't pay me, sir. I pay you, a shilling a year – for the privilege of being your piper sir."

"Oh, really?" Duncan wore a relieved smile. "And why are you playing here this morning, Lachlan?"

"Do you not know what day it is, sir?"

"Er, Sunday."

"Aye, but what day is it?"

"November 30th. Isn't it?"

"And every true Scotsman knows what day November 30th is," said Lachlan.

"St Andrew's Day! St Andrew is the Patron Saint of Scotland."

Lachlan beamed. "That it is, sir. That it is. Scotland's national day, and every November thirtieth, it's the duty of the Laird of Airde's piper to play the pipes at the castle gate at dawn, to welcome in St Andrew's day, come rain, hail or shine."

"Well won't you come inside and have breakfast with us?"

"That's very kind of you, sir. I don't mind if I do."

Duncan led the way in toward the warm air and cooking smells from the kitchen, and called out to Jean in a happy voice, that their first real guest had arrived. He seemed not to notice the border collie dog at the piper's heel slip inside as the kilted Scotsman walked across the threshold. The dog padded quietly over to one of the grandfather chairs by the fireplace, hopped onto it, and curled up, as if it belonged there.

The children, now dressed in their warm dressing-gowns and slippers, stood in a line by the fireplace, like a welcoming committee to greet the Scottish piper, eyes agog at how splendid Lachlan looked.

At the sight of the beautiful collie dog, they each shared a look of amazement, one to the other, but daren't say anything. For each one of them, had for so long, wanted a dog of their very own, but their parents had been against it. So they were astonished when this very fine-looking dog wondered in, and made himself completely at home, without a challenge from either their mother or their father!

"This is young Lachlan MacGregor, Jean," said Duncan, hanging up his outdoor attire on a hallstand. "He's the young man the Ghillie told us about." Then he went on to explain to Jean that Lachlan was now their personal piper and would join them for breakfast.

Lachlan, a strapping lad with magnificently chiselled features smiled broadly at the family. "It's mighty grand of you. Mrs Campbell. I'd be honoured to share a meal with you." He shook her hand, then turned to face the children. "And who have we here?" As their father introduced each child in turn, Lachlan shook each child's hand.

"Come warm yourself by the fire, Lachlan," said Jean.

After laying down his tartan tam o'shanter – his bonnet, with an adornment of tassles and pheasant feathers, he unstrapped his bagpipes. And as he laid his treasure on a nearby bench, air escaped from its tartan bag, travelled through the wooden pipes, then it let out a groan, and a pitiful, agonizing wail. And, as if to add an encore, it finished with a most peculiar, high-pitched squeak. He turned and grinned at little Dottie. "Sometimes, I think there's a funny wee man in there."

Dottie got a fit of the giggles. Then Katie caught it, and as much as Robert tried to fight it, he too found himself chuckling, and before long, the whole family was laughing, with Lachlan joining in.

The Campbells from Australia had found a new Scottish friend.

#

It was mid-morning by the time Lachlan rose to go, after much food and good humour. He had duties to attend to in the village, but he promised to return and repair the broken slates on the castle's old roof as soon as the weather permitted. He also promised Robert, that he would one day soon, teach him how to play the bagpipes.

The family all stood at the castle entrance to bid their new friend farewell, when Duncan, out of the blue, shouted after the young man. "Don't forget your lovely dog, Lachlan."

"But he's not my dog, Mr Campbell," answered the lad as he waved another goodbye, before marching off back down toward the village, bagpipes on his shoulder. The happy skirl was heard yet again, this time a famous, jaunty, uplifting tune as he tramped on his way. It was called, 'Scotland The Brave.'

The family returned inside, talking and laughing about all the things Lachlan had told them. About the village, the people, and all the wonderful new experiences they could expect from 'Bonnie Scotland,' its customs, and its folklore. All but Katie had returned inside. Katie remained at the great front door watching the dashing young Highlander depart, as fresh new snow began to fall and cover the black footsteps that her father and Lachlan had made on its pristine cloak of snow.

Katie watched Lachlan for a long moment, dreamily, and listened as the haunting melody wafted through the eery air of stillness; she watched until he began to fade out of sight, into the magic mist of snow; as if he'd been nothing more than an illusion.

Then something very strange occurred to Katie. The dog which had come to visit with Lachlan, had not left any paw prints in the snow.

Chapter 6

Eyes moist with emotion after pleading his case, with promises of care and responsibility, Robert was highly elated, when told that the mysterious, and beautiful, collie dog could stay.

With his arm wrapped lovingly, protectively around the collie's neck, Robert looked deep into its dark brown doggie eyes, and declared that his name was now 'Scottie' no matter what it had been before. And that very same day he began teaching Scottie tricks.

And what a clever dog Scottie turned out to be. Robert only had to tell him something once. Just once, and he understood. It was as if he were a human in disguise. Robert couldn't believe his luck. To find a new friend like Scottie, a trusted friend, a brave friend, a loyal friend, and especially such a smart one, made Robert's life with his two sisters such a whole lot better. The two became inseparable. It made Katie's life easier, too. Robert wasn't teasing her so much now that he was occupied with his new friend.

"Now, Scottie," Robert said seriously one day to his canine companion, as they played catch in the 200 foot long empty ballroom. "I have something very special in mind for us." Scottie trotted back with the wooden porridge stirrer in his mouth that they'd been using. "Mum and Dad need some help with the family finances, so this idea of mine will be our contribution, and we can have some fun at the same time."

Scottie dropped the foot-long porridge stirrer at Robert's feet beside the Frisbee and the tennis ball, and gave out a glorious 'Woof.'

"Now, I'm sure you won't mind," said Robert, "but you'll be required to wear an outfit. A white outfit, and prance around in the dark. Okay?" He raised his eyebrows, dropped his chin, and gave his new pal an intense questioning look. Scottie jumped up and licked him on the cheek. "I think the library would be a good place to find a ghost, don't you? I'm sure ghosts are 'booky' – spooky booky," he grinned, and Scottie barked in agreement. "Or, way down in the dungeon, down the steps at the end of the dark, south wing; oh... and up in the garret. It's really spooky in there, Scottie." Scottie barked in agreement, and Robert rubbed his hands together with glee. "Whoooooooo!" He demonstrated a spooky moan to emphasise his point. "What do you think?"

Scottie let out a sharp little yap, and Robert gave him a hug.

"Great. Now, here's what we're going to do. We'll have a few practice runs - just you and me - before we include the girls, okay?" To which Scottie responded with a resounding 'Woof,' with Robert responding to that, with a generous pat, as the two headed off in the direction of Jean Campbell's linen cupboard to borrow a white sheet.

Meanwhile, Katie, also aware of the family financial difficulties, had been trying to teach little Dottie to knit mittens to sell in the village. But after only one lesson, she was forced to admit that it was a futile exercise. Little Dottie just couldn't manage to hold the knitting needles. Then Katie tried to teach her how to make pretty new Christmas cards. Christmas was only three weeks away, so she got straight to work. But with blunt baby scissors it was all much too difficult for the tot.

Then, Katie had the bright idea that they should make Christmas decorations, with crepe paper, bubble-wrap and the milk bottle tops she'd been saving. And Dottie was doing a great job stringing all the silver tops together, but she soon lost interest, and was quick to scamper off, leaving Katie to work by herself.

So, while Duncan worked assiduously in his office trying to catch up on his backlog of work, and Jean and Effie baked a generous supply of Christmas cakes and puddings to sell, a secret, ghostly business enterprise to increase family funds, was put into action by Robert and his new canine friend, Scottie.

Quietly, stealthily, creeping up the stairs, and past Katie's bedroom, fleet, and light of foot, Robert and Scottie were headed toward the library, when a voice startled them.

"And where do you think you're going with Mum's best damask bedspread, Robert Campbell? You're up to something, and I want to know what it is," the voice demanded.

Robert and his trusty friend turned sheepishly around to see Katie standing with hands on hips like an admonishing school-teacher. "Oh... er, I, er..." They shared a guilty look.

"Come on, Robert, out with it." She raised an eyebrow. "And don't tell me any fibs. You certainly weren't about to iron it, or anything useful like that! You can't make a tent with Mum's best linen you know!"

Caught in the act, and rooted to the spot, the two conspirators remained silent. With heads bowed.

"Tell me what you're up to, or I'll tell mum!"

Chapter 7

During a clandestine phone call, Robert and Katie had made arrangements to meet with Lachlan MacGregor. They had agreed, as a team, that they would need help from a friendly grown-up to make their scheme the very best that it could be. So with that in mind, they made arrangements to go with their father Duncan, the very next time he went to the village, at which time they could visit, and discuss their confidential plan with the friendly Scot.

"Now this is what we need," began Robert, in a very grown-up manner, when they sat conferring with Lachlan at his workshop. As was the way now, everywhere that Robert went, Scottie went too. Scottie sat at his feet and wagged his tail now and again during the visit, as the details were discussed. "But we can't afford to pay you, Lachlan, until we get our first busload of customers."

Lachlan, a carpenter and joiner by trade, with his own growing business in Airde, smiled warmly at the youngsters. He stood at his workbench dressed in blue overalls tucked into heavy leather boots, wearing a thick, fairisle jumper beneath that his mother had knitted, and a bright red tammy perched on the side of his head. "Whatever it is that you're needing, young Robert, I'll be only too happy to help you," he said in response, pleased that the youngsters were asking him for help.

"We would like you to make a couple of road signs for us, Lachlan," said Katie sweetly, looking up into his kindly face.

"And we'll pay you the proper amount of course," said Robert, as soon as we get some customers."

Which Katie repeated, to show how honest, and ethical, they intended to be in this business arrangement, "Yes, as soon as we get some customers!"

"And when do you want these signs?" Lachlan asked.

"We thought," said Robert, "if you could do them by the end of the day..."

"Oh, you're not in a hurry then!" Lachlan responded with a laugh, as he looked from one to the other of their innocent faces, etched as they were with disarmingly pleading expressions.

"We're going to have Castle Airde Ghost Tours for the tourists," Robert announced.

"Aah!" Lachlan hid his grin with a make-believe cough, hand over his mouth.

"It's going to solve all mum and dad's money worries," Kate nodded with affirmation.

"It was my idea," said Robert proudly.

"Is that so?" Lachlan said thoughtfully, crossing his muscly arms, and resting back on his work bench. "Well now, as you are my very first customers from Down Under, I'll make an arrangement with you. Build now – pay later."

"You will?" The pair said in unison.

"You'll know of course, that a Scotsman aye keeps his word, so, you just tell me how many signs you want, and how big you want them, and what you want painted on them. Tell me where you want them to go, and the job will be done before the sun sets tonight."

"It will?"

"Aye, that it will," said Lachlan, giving the two bright-eyed youngsters a broad smile. "I see it as a very good business proposition, you understand. Because it's very obvious to me, that I'll be doing quite a bit of business in the future, with two such enterprising entrepreneurs." He unlocked his arms and held out a big strong hand to them. "Shake on it, partners."

41

As the children, each in turn vigorously shook Lachlan's hand, Scottie gave a 'Woof' of approval.

#

Although the outside temperature still hovered close to zero, Mother Nature had decided she would keep her best snowfalls till a later date. She had sent only her frostiest, yet brightest of days, and despite the children being a little disappointed that they could not yet build a snowman, or have a good-natured snowball fight, or skate on the lake, or sledge down the hillsides, they were happy that the many pre-Christmas tasks that came with the season, were well under way. Best of all, they had two full weeks to make a few extra pennies with their Ghost Tours.

"Ready?" said Robert to Katie, Dottie, and Scottie, when he thought he had his ghostly plan polished to perfection, and was ready to demonstrate it in the castle library. They had brought little Dottie in on the plan too, by this time, because even she could play a part in the Castle Airde Ghost Tours.

"Ready!" the girls confirmed.

'Woof' barked Scottie.

"Okay. Tell mum and dad that they can come in now."

Summoned by their daughters, Jean and Duncan Campbell eventually gave in to their children's pleas, but under protest, because each had been busy with their own tasks.

"Is this going to take long, kids?" Duncan queried. "I've got a lot of work to do in the office."

"And I have pies in the oven," said Jean with a frown. "Now what's this secret of yours? I don't like my time being wasted, or my pies burning."

"Oh, please, mum," said Katie, tugging at her mother's hand as she pulled her into the long, narrow library, where the shelves were lined with books from floor to ceiling. Books of every size, leather bound mostly, and very old indeed. This well-stocked library had an ornate wooden mezzanine floor, twenty feet up in the air, like a balcony, which went all the way around it. And the books were stacked so high, that long ladders had to be used to reach them.

This was to be the last dress rehearsal of the scheme - for their parent's benefit - before tourists came. Tomorrow would be the real thing. Lachlan's signs would be on display along the main road to the village by morning, directing passing tourists to the castle for The Ghost Tours.

"Everybody in position," came Robert's voice from up on the mezzanine floor, and his two sisters scampered away, leaving their parents standing bemused, at the entrance to the dark library. Robert put a hand-made paper megaphone to his lips, and read from a handwritten script. "Ladies and gentlemen, welcome to Castle Airde Ghost Tours. This castle dates from the thirteenth century, and has been built, and rebuilt, many times down throughout the ages. There were many fires which damaged the castle, and, there were many fierce battles. It is said to have many ghosts of brave soldiers who fought to keep it."

Jean and Duncan looked at each other and smiled.

Robert flicked off a light switch and the library was suddenly enveloped in darkness. Then Robert pushed the 'play' button of his father's tape recorder, and it began to play a tape of 'ghostly' noises, which he, Katie and Dottie had great fun recording during the afternoon, 'groaning' and 'oooooing', and 'aaaaahhhhhing', and rattling old bells and chains. With a snigger or two in-between. "The ghost of William Wallace the great warrior himself, is said to inhabit these halls. But one of the most famous ghosts of all, is Horace The Hunchback of Castle Airde."

He gave Scottie a nudge forward into the darkness, then flicked on his father's biggest torch. He shone the beam on the collie who was clad in a white bedsheet, with a cardboard box strapped on his back. In the glow of the torch, the Campbells watched as the clever dog came scampering down the staircase from the mezzanine, till Robert was heard to whisper to him. Then Scottie slowed to a snail's pace – to make it look more authentic - because that is how ghosts are known to move. Slowly. When Scottie reached the bottom, Robert whistled softly, and Scottie turned and slowly climbed back up again, with his paws protruding from beneath the sheet, making him, sadly, a very unconvincing ghost, despite the morbid ghost noises.

"Oh, dear, my good clean linen," Jean exclaimed.

"Another famous ghost of Castle Airde," continued Robert, switching off the torch, is Friar Fortescue, the Headless Monk. He died when the castle was besieged - after the defeat of Bonnie Prince Charlie - and who, still today, roams the castle's corridors walls and turrets – headlessly." Again he switched on the tape-recorder, then the torch, and this time focused its beam on the door behind his parents.

Both Jean and Duncan turned to see the library door slowly open, with a squeal and a moan. And then a tall, white, headless figure entered, making wailing sounds. But suddenly the figure stumbled on the uneven stone floor, and with a cry of alarm, its top half fell off, and the entire figure crumbled in a heap on the floor.

Hurrying to the pile of arms and legs, Jean and Duncan pulled away a white bedsheet to reveal their two daughters sprawled on the stone floor with little Dottie on the verge of tears.

"Robert, turn on the lights, and turn off that dreadful racket!" Duncan commanded. And come down here at once and explain yourself."

The enterprising youngster knew by the tone of his father's voice that he was in big trouble.

"Yes, Dad," he sighed.

When Robert and Scottie joined the others downstairs, they could see a big lump on Dottie's forehead, and Jean giving her a comforting cuddle.

"Dottie fall long way down!" the infant whimpered.

"I didn't mean to tumble, Dottie," said Katie unhappily. "I tripped. I'm sorry!"

"So, what's all this Ghost Tour nonsense, Robert?" Duncan demanded.

"We thought we might be able to help make some money for you Dad," Robert explained.

"Oh, aren't you little darlings," said their mother proudly.

It was enough to touch their father's heart, too. He couldn't be very angry with his boy now. "Well," said Duncan, clearing his throat, "that was very good of the three of you."

"Four, Daddy," Dottie corrected her father, when Scottie jumped up to lick her tear-stained cheek. Dottie knew her numbers up to twenty, and was quick to include Scottie.

"Okay, four of you. But I think it would take a little more than this to make a Ghost Tour, kids."

Jean checked to see that no-one was badly hurt, then she and Duncan led them out of the library, extinguished the light, and pulled shut the library door, to return to her cooking in the kitchen.

But no sooner had they closed the library door behind them, than they heard the sound of bagpipes playing a rousing march, and it was getting louder and louder. Then they heard the beating of drums from some far off place, and the thud of hundreds of marching feet, getting closer and closer. The volume itself was frightening. They looked to one another in absolute horror. They were rooted to the spot.

An ear-splitting war-cry was heard, and the clamour of an ancient battle met their ears. The clang of metal on metal, the clash of sword and shield, the whinnying of terrified horses, the cries of wounded men. A real life battle seemed to be taking place in the

45

castle library, right behind the door. The realistic sounds sent a chill down the spines of each member of the Campbell family.

"What the devil is that?" queried Duncan, swinging back to look at the library door, his heart beating fast within his manly chest. But, being the head of the family, he knew he could show no fear in front of the children. So, bravely, he reached out, and, tremulously turned the old handle, and flung open the door as if the handle was hot, and with that, silence returned. The room was empty, and not a sound could be heard.

The Campbell family huddled together at the library entrance, and stared into the vast space, and waited. Just waited. But nothing happened.

"It must have been the tape recorder," said Jean.

"Must have been," Duncan agreed. "I thought I told you to turn it off, Robert?"

"I did, Dad! I really did!"

"I think you ought to check it again, son," said Duncan, doubting him.

Baffled by the blood-curdling noises that Robert was sure he didn't make, he never-the-less went to check the tape-recording machine back up on the mezzanine floor. When he reached the top, he checked it and found, that sure enough, it was in the off position, and neither he, nor Katie could explain the mysterious noises. No-one except little Dottie. She tugged at her father's sleeve.

"What is it, Dottie?" said Duncan, looking down at her.

"Big Man," she said, pointing back towards the library. "My Big Man, Daddy."

With a smile Duncan bent down and picked up his little bundle of joy, saying, "You and your imaginary 'Big Man,'" he chuckled to himself. "If there really was an invisible 'Big Man' in this castle, then your Ghost Tours might just stand a ghost of a chance of succeeding!"

At supper time, with the family sitting at the long table in the kitchen in front of a roaring fire, just finishing their meal, Duncan decided to get something off his chest.

"About these ghost tours, Robert. I know that your intentions were honourable. What I mean is, I know that you were trying to help your mother and me, but for ghost tours, you need real ghosts. And as we don't happen to have any..." he shrugged. "See what I'm getting at, son?"

"But everyone knows that castles are haunted," Robert protested.

"That's no reason to try to trick people," his father responded. "I know you're not a cheat, Robert, so we'll forget the idea, will we?"

"Yeees, Dad," Robert answered with a sigh. "Can I leave the table now?"

"Yes, you may. But I want no more fraudulent schemes!"

Robert swung his legs around from the long bench, feeling frustrated. He hurried off to his bedroom to think about things, feeling a bit dejected at his plan not succeeding, and being scolded into the bargain. He had a scowl on his face, leaving his father shaking his head.

Robert was sad, and confused. His plan had been to help his family. Everyone knew there wasn't any such thing as a ghost. They were only on TV and in the movies. So anyone who came on the Castle Airde Ghost Tour would know they were only pretend ghosts. Like at the Haunted House at Disneyland. Everyone just went there for the fun of it. As far as Robert was concerned, if you gave people what they wanted to see, that wasn't really cheating.

#

Next morning, Robert told his father that he would cycle down to the main road and remove the Ghost Tour signs. So, with Scottie sitting in a specially built doggie-trailer fitted behind the back wheel – custom made for him by Lachlan, and lined with tartan wool carpet – a rugged-up Robert headed down to the village. He loved to traverse the dark tunnels at break-neck speed. He followed the arrows and turned the tight, dark bends, and pretended that he was a race-car driver driving in the Grand Prix.

The cold wind stung his cheeks as he exited the winding tunnels, to tackle the next stage of his journey on the open road. The sturdy steed took Robert and Scottie down the rest of the steep decline at super-sonic speed without incident. And, as he wound down and around the narrow road, he frequently freed his feet from the pedals on the straight stretches and free-wheeled. Here, he pretended he was a flying ace. Scottie, with jaw open, and his long pink tongue hanging out, sat in his cosy trailer at the back, with a look of contentment on his happy, windswept face.

If Lachlan had kept his word, thought Robert, a sign should have been strategically placed at the junction of the village and castle road. But when Robert arrived at the bottom of the hill, he found no Ghost Tour sign at the junction.

"That's strange, Scottie," said Robert to his best mate, as he stood at the fork in the road, one leg on a bicycle peddle, the other on the ground. "Lachlan promised us he'd put the signs up last night. Let's go check the one on the main road to the village."

"Woof."

And off they went to the right, along the narrow road to the junction of the village road, and the Highland's main road, travelling alongside the icy, silvery lake. This time with great care, for he knew that other vehicles shared this stretch. Soon, he came to the section of road which ran along beside the property of the rude, unfriendly Major Fordyce. There should have been a sign here, too, but there wasn't. Robert was perplexed. He could not believe that Lachlan would fail to keep his word.

Just then, he heard a 'toot, toot, toot,' and looking around, he saw a long, low, yellow car coming out of Major Fordyce's gate. It was an old-fashioned Morgan sports car, with wire wheels and big black mud-guards. The matronly woman driver was waving back over her shoulder to Major Fordyce, who looked as if he was holding one of Robert's Ghost Tour signs under his arm. And Fordyce was beaming like a Cheshire Cat as he waved the woman a fond farewell. The Morgan went on toward the village with more tooting of horn, as the driver went on her way.

Robert's foot went back on the bicycle pedal and he made a sweeping turn, to take off after the sporty vehicle at full speed, intending to follow and find out what she was up to. And although Scottie barked his encouragement as they sped along the narrow road, that wound round the foot of purple-heathered hillsides, with the tranquil water of Loch Airde to one side, the jaunty yellow Morgan soon disappeared from sight. Try as Robert might, his legs were no match for its big V8 engine.

He headed down the last stretch leading to the outskirts of the village, where he expected to see the third and last sign. Sure enough there it was, tacked to a roadside power pole. And there too, was the yellow Morgan – it had come to a halt right beside the sign. And the plump woman driver had stopped and was alighting the vehicle.

He slowed to a halt and watched as the woman walked up to the sign and proceeded to rip it down.

"Hey! You can't do that!" he yelled, but to no avail. The woman turned, giggled like a schoolgirl, stuck her chin in the air, then got back into the car taking the sign with her. With a roar the engine started up, and the car drove off.

"Did you see that, Scottie? Who gave her the right to do that?" Robert said with disbelief. "She must have taken the other signs down too. Come on, let's find Lachlan."

#

"A yellow Morgan, you say? Oh, that would be Marjory Meddle," said Lachlan, when Robert found him working in his village workshop. "Mother Meddle," we call her. She meddles in everybody's business. They say she has too much time on her hands, now that Montgomery, her husband, is no longer with us."

"But what would she have against our signs?"

"Oh, well now, I'd imagine that she's just trying to please Major Fordyce. He'd be the one with the grumble. He doesn't like the tourists, as you know. And of course the tourist coaches have to pass by his property to get into Airde."

"Is there any other way they can get to the village or the castle, Lachlan?"

"I'm afraid not, Robert, m'boy. Afraid not," Lachlan said sadly. "It was a good try, but it looks like you'll have to think up another wee money-making scheme for your parents. For, as fast as we made new signs, old Mother Meddle would just take them down again."

"We could call the police, couldn't we, Lachlan? She's stealing our property!"

"Ah, well," said Lachlan with a sigh, "strictly speaking, it's against the By-laws to put signs up at the roadside. Technically, Robert, I'm afraid that Marjory Meddle and the Major are in the right."

"What if I was to ask the Major to let us keep the signs up?" suggested Robert innocently.

"You'd be wasting your breath, Robert. Wasting your breath. He's not a generous man." Lachlan gave Robert an

50

encouraging pat on his shoulder, as he was very much aware of his disappointment. "It was a good try. Very enterprising."

Not one to be defeated easily, Robert told Lachlan that he would take a ride down by the lake to think over the situation. A good hard think in private, had helped in the past to come up with alternative solutions.

#

A thick, lazy mist hung over the southern end of icy Loch Beiste, on this silvery grey day as Robert sat with his trusty friend by his side, on a large flat-topped rock at the water's edge, and his bicycle at the ready, nearby. All was silent and still, but for the gentle lapping of water on the rocks and pebbles, with only the occasional plop of a fish surfacing briefly out in the lake.

Robert spoke his thoughts while Scottie listened. Not that Robert really needed an answer, or guidance, he just needed company. And Scottie sat close up against his friend to keep him warm, for although the sun shone weakly, and the air was still, there was a chilling edge to it.

"We have to help Mum and Dad, somehow, Scottie. We have to save the castle. If we can't pay our way, then we'll have to leave. And I'd be sad, because I like it here. I like going to school here. I want to grow up here." He was quiet for a moment, and stared into the waters of the great lake as he sorted out his thoughts. "I've made lots of new friends here. Like Lachlan, and you." He gave his favourite chum a pat and ruffled his collar. "I miss some things about Australia, but... I like this new life here. How many kids get to live in their very own castle?"

"Woof!"

Scottie sat beside him panting, with his long pink tongue hanging out, and his hot breath steaming on the cold morning air.

Robert grinned at him. "You look like a dragon sitting there with all that steam coming out of your mouth, Scottie."

"Woof!"

"Yes, you do buddy," he chortled, cuddling into his faithful companion. "A fiery dragon." Robert blew his own hot breath out into the cold air to compare, then he studied it absently as it drifted off into nothing on the cold air.

Suddenly, he spied something moving in the water. A big, dark thing, which glided silently through the icy lake, leaving a spreading wake, which fanned out behind it. "Look, Scottie – in the lake, something's out there. It looks like a slithering serpent." But his excitement was soon quashed when a boat's horn blasted and he realised that it was only a fishing boat.

Scottie gave out a sharp bark as if he were trying to tell Robert something, then he jumped from the rock they were sitting on, and bounded away, disappearing behind a great round boulder further along the water's edge.

"Scottie, what are you up to? Come on out from there." The boy laughed at his companion's funny antics. All he could see was Scottie's dragon-like breath coming out from behind the boulder. "Wait a minute... that gives me an idea!"

He shot to his feet as if he had been struck by a bolt of lightning. Triumphantly, he shouted. "That's it, Scottie. That's it boy, of course! What we need is a MONSTER!" Eyes wide with excitement at his stroke of genius. "We need a monster – like the Loch Ness Monster! Here! At Lake Airde!" He looked over at his furry friend.

Scottie's head peered from around the boulder to look at Robert.

"A LOCH BEISTE MONSTER! That's what we need, Scottie!"

"Woof, Woof, Woof," Scottie barked, and came bounding up to Robert and began to chase his tail in celebration. Round and round and round he went, trying to catch it, looking like a fluffy spinning top.

"Come on, Scottie," Robert said excitedly, springing into action, he jumped down and whisked up his bicycle. We're going straight back to see Lachlan!"

"Woof!"

Chapter 8

Not even a pretty young woman could distract Lachlan MacGregor, as, with sparks flying, he welded with an oxy-acetylene torch in his workshop. So Mary Sinclair, the bright young Scottish lass, with a peaches and cream complexion who came to visit him, had to tap him on the shoulder for attention. He stopped welding, pushed back his faceguard, and gave her a grand smile.

"Hello, Lachlan," smiled Mary, right back at him. Mary was a 'stringer,' a writer, who worked now and then for national newspapers when a good news story broke in their area. Mary, a pretty girl, and a decent lass, had a keen mind and a cheery disposition.

Thinking that he must look like the Australian bushranger, Ned Kelly, in his protective helmet, Lachlan extinguished his torch for safety's sake, and removed his bulky head gear, ready to talk to his visitor.

"Hello there, Mary. What brings you to a man's place of work this fine day?" He leaned back against his workbench the way he always did when he lay down his tools, and stopped to talk.

"I'm sorry to bother you, Lachlan, but I'm here on a spying mission," she answered with just a hint of mischief in her voice.

Lachlan grinned a great, broad grin. "A spying mission, you say, Mary?"

"Yes. Someone rang *The Edinburgh Rocket* and told them that our Major Fordyce is personally responsible for holding back the economy of the Scottish Highlands, because he won't allow tourist coaches into the village."

Lachlan couldn't help but smile. He could guess where such a call came from. He'd bet it was a young lad by the name of Robert, whose best friend was a collie dog. "Is that so, Mary?" he answered as innocently as his conscience would allow.

"Yes, Lachlan, so I came to see you, and talk to you about it first, so that I could get the truth of the matter, before I go off to face that nasty piece of work, Fordyce."

"Well now, Mary," Lachlan said, his eyes alight with devilment. "I'll make a bargain with you, being the canny lad that I am." He used a Scottish word that meant being careful, and a little bit cunning, like a fox. "If you were to promise me, that you'll save the last dance for me, at the Laird's Hogmanay party on New Year's Eve, then I'll tell you what that Major Fordyce has been up to."

"Oh, I see," Mary returned. "You've put a price upon the truth have you then, Lachlan?" She gave her handsome friend a cheeky grin.

"There's a price for everything, Mary, lass," said Lachlan, grinning, and taking off his thick work gloves. "Come and sit yourself down, and we'll have a nice hot cup of tea while we talk."

"Thank you, Lachlan. I knew I could depend on you."

"Here, let me help you over," he said, and he stretched out a strong hand to help Mary through a tangle of wood, metal and machinery, which lay strewn about the concrete floor in her path.

"What kind of a monstrous thing is this you're making now, Lachlan?" she asked, grasping hold of his outstretched hand, and looking deep into his eyes for more of the truth.

Hesitating to answer, Lachlan first gave out a little cough to clear his throat, and give him time to think before replying. "It is a wee bit monstrous looking, I'll grant you that, Mary," he smiled. "But, er, it's just a clever mechanical bit of machinery that I'm building for a special client. It hasn't got a name."

Mary looked at him suspiciously. Her well-trained journalistic mind told her that something 'fishy' was going on. "And is that a wet-suit I see hanging up, at this time of year, Lachlan? Surely you're not diving in the lake in this weather?"

"Oh, that, Mary... I, er, was just checking it for wee holes. Getting it ready for my next job, you might say. Just checking it, Mary."

"Then why is it all wet, Lachlan?" she asked with a raised brow and a steely gaze.

"Now how else would I check it for holes, Mary?" he returned with a grin.

"Lachlan MacGregor," Mary began in school-teacher fashion, "I might be young, and I might be a female, but let me tell you, that I am not in the least bit stupid! I know when somebody's up to something. And I can smell something fishy going on here. And I'll get to the bottom of it. You just wait and see if I don't!"

"Now then, Mary, you know you have a wee bit of trouble controlling that imagination of yours," he grinned, with a twinkle in his eye.

"If I'm imagining things Lachlan, then what's that oxygen tank out for?" She pointed to the cylinder which allowed him to breath under water. "All I can say, Lachlan, is that it must be something that's either very important, or very daft to take you into that freezing lake at this time of year!"

"Oh, it is that, Mary. It is that," he smiled.

"Which? Important, or daft?" she said, eyes twinkling.

"Take your pick, Mary. Now, will you have a cup of tea with me?"

"Lachlan MacGregor you are impossible!" Mary laughed.

#

Major Fordyce's slavering dog Magnus growled ferociously as it lay at his master's feet, with a perpetual drip of gooey thick saliva hanging from its slimy jaw. A low, menacing growl it was, like a rumbling volcano which might erupt at any moment.

In the major's sitting room, a dark and scary place, guns were mounted on every wall, alongside the trophies of his horrid killing sports; a swordfish, over four metres long was mounted on a plaque, various sized deer antlers, a stuffed eagle, a shell of a giant turtle, ostrich eggs, and the terrifying, gaping jaws of an Indian tiger, with fangs as long as knitting needles, and worst of all, the magnificent ivory tusks of an African elephant.

Mary Sinclair sat nervously on the edge of her chair opposite the dreaded man himself, with pen poised, her notebook on her knee, writing down every angry word that erupted from the grisly old man's mouth.

"I will not have coaches full of outsiders trooping in and out of my village," he declared, with Magnus maintaining his gurgling growl, his eyes set firmly on the nervous Mary Sinclair. "And you can tell that to your newspaper readers!" The major went on huffing and puffing about the need for peace and quiet. He spat and spluttered more furiously by the minute. And the more animated he became, the more he seemed to Mary, to look like his dog Magnus.

"But," Mary began her argument meekly, trying to get a word in without upsetting the miserly man, "surely all you need to do, Major Fordyce," she said as sweetly as she could, "is let the tourist coaches drive past? You need never know that they're there. They needn't disturb you. The business people of the village would benefit from an influx of tourists."

"I'll give them influx! I will not have it, young lady!" Fordyce bellowed.

"Shouldn't we move with the times, Major?"

"Time stands still in a place like Airde, and that's the way I like it, girl. I came here for peace and quiet, and that's what I expect. I will not have outsiders and foreigners invading my village. And that's that!" With clenched fist he pounded the arm of his chair to make his point. And with his thunderous outburst, the ugly dog growled louder, and deeper, and showed Mary more of his formidable sharp teeth, while heavy drips of slimy saliva dropped onto the carpet.

"Er, then may I take a photograph of you, Major Fordyce?" asked Mary politely, realising that no-one could reason with such a selfish, inflexible man. "For the newspaper article."

"Possibly, possibly. But not now, girlie," he said, dismissively. "Not now. Tomorrow morning when I go into the village to collect my fresh Forfar Bridies from the widow Meddle. Bakes them especially for me, you know."

What the Major didn't say, was that he would be looking his best when he went to visit the widow Marjory Meddle in the morning, and only his best would do for the camera.

"I don't mind posing down by the shores of Loch Beiste," he declared, with a good dose of conceit. "That would be the perfect setting – a peaceful location. These Highlands of ours are a private place, and I'm going to see that they stay that way. It's bad enough having to put up with those damned Australians up at the castle! Do you understand me, girlie?"

"Yes, sir, I do. But, Major Fordyce, don't you think that the Scottish Highlands are the most beautiful place on earth? All of Scotland sees them that way, and so do millions of people right around the world. Don't you think we should share their magic with the rest of the world?"

"Sharing is an overrated concept to my mind. Only a fool gives away what's rightfully his." He rose to his feet as fast as his clumsy fat body would allow, then Magnus rose up, first on his hind legs, then on his front paws in a clumsy waddle motion to find his balance. "I served my Queen and country in the army, and purchased my property here for peace and quiet in my retirement. That's what I want! And that's what I'll get."

Mary noticed Magnus take a determined step closer toward her. Panting hungrily now, and seeming to lick his lips as if he were about to gobble dinner.

She stood her ground. "Yes, Major F..."

But before she could finish her response, Fordyce pronounced that he would be down by MacTaggart's Landing, opposite the Village Green, at midday next day, and if Mary wanted to take his photograph for *The Edinburgh Rocket*, then she'd best be there at that time.

Chapter 9

Chocolates. Toffees. Licorice allsorts. Edinburgh rock. Coconut Ice. Fudge. Crème caramels. Fruit pastels. Jelly babies. And much much more. The tiny sweet-smelling Airde Village sweetie shop was a paradise for children. And every one of the wonderful delicacies had been lovingly hand-made by ninety-nine year-old Rosemary Robertson who had been born and raised right there in the village.

"There you are, my bonnie wee bairns," she said to the Campbell children who had been given pocket-money for Christmas, and had headed straight for the quaint old sweet shop. "I've popped in a few of my delicious Strawberry Kisses, from me to you, for Christmas," said the little old lady as she smiled down cheerfully at Robert, Katie, and little Dottie, from her specially built platform at the other side of the counter. A wooden platform, that went right around the U-shaped counter, which had been custom-made for her by Lachlan MacGregor.

You see, Miss Robertson was not as much as four feet tall, and in the past when she had tried to serve her customers, no one could tell where her sweet little voice was coming from, until Lachlan had suggested making the elevated platform for her. And now, she could reach her sweetie jars on either side.

"Thank you, Miss Robertson," the Campbell children chorused gratefully, their faces beaming. They turned, waved her a fond farewell, wished her a merry Christmas, and headed out to find their parents who were completing their Christmas shopping at Walter Wriggly's bookstore, 'The Wriggly Bookworm,' across the Village Green.

It was nearly midday, and there was excitement in the air, with only a few days left before Christmas was upon them. And the Village Hall clock, which had been newly repaired by Lachlan, would soon chime out the hour with twelve, ear-splitting booms. Booms louder than Big Ben booms. More like supersonic booms, shattering the peace of the village. And people everywhere would put their hands over their ears, and shake their heads.

Past the baker's shop the Campbell children went, it's delicious aromas wafting out into the crisp clean Highland air making them hungry. Wonderful aromas of freshly baked bread, and mouth-watering cakes and biscuits, like melting moments, shortbread fingers, gingerbread men, doughnuts, blueberry muffins, and a specialty at this time of year, fruit mince pies.

Then, past the barber's shop they went. The barber was kept busy tidying beards for the Christmas season, and it was a crowded, happy place, for the barber and his three assistants sang together as they worked, to make a barber-shop quartet. Then on past the boatman who had been building a replica of Noah's Ark in his spare time for as long as anyone could remember.

Past the busy blacksmith, who, with muscles bulging, made horse-shoes and nails, and wrought-iron ornaments in his forge, and never felt the cold with his hot furnace glowing from inside his dark burrow of a workplace. Past the post office which was extremely busy this time of year, sending and delivering parcels; and then on to the butcher's shop with Scottie bounding on ahead barking expectantly, for he had been promised a juicy bone.

The old stone buildings around the Village Green were festooned with bright Christmas decorations. Roasting chestnuts sizzled on an open fire where the older villagers had gathered to drink Hot Toddies to keep warm. The Airde Village Children's Choir was grouped around the base of a magnificent Christmas tree, singing 'Jingle Bells.' They looked resplendent in old-fashioned red capes and boots and pom-pom hats as their angelic

61

voices sent out a loving message of goodwill to all men, and women – even to the grumpy Major Fordyce.

A team of the cutest Shetland ponies came prancing by, the bells tied round their necks jingling a happy, melodious tune as they paraded. They pulled a neat white carriage festooned with red ribbons and bows. Inside was Santa, who smiled and gave cheer, joyously throwing brightly coloured bon-bons to the children of the village. Like all the other youngsters, the Campbell children waved as he went by, with little Dottie jumping up and down in her excitement. Robert didn't like to tell her it was only the Ghillie dressed up. He knew that the real Santa would pay them a visit on Christmas Eve.

A gentle sprinkling of snow began to fall and cover the ground with a talcum-powder coating, making the scene look pristine pure.

"Hope this snow keeps up, Katie," said Robert, his eyes dancing with mischief. "Then we can throw snowballs at old Major Fordyce for sending Mother Meddle to take down our signs. I'd love to knock his silly, deer-stalker hat off!"

"Robert! You'd better not let Mum and Dad hear you talk like that!" Katie scolded.

"Well, what do you expect I should feel about the Major? Should I send him some Strawberry Kisses?" Robert laughed. "Just wait, Katie Campbell. Have I got a surprise for him!" Then he took off and ran across the Village Green.

The word had quickly gotten around that Major Fordyce was to meet Mary Sinclair down at MacTaggart's Landing at midday, and Katie felt sure that was where Robert was headed. She whisked little Dottie up in her arms and ran as fast as she could after her brother.

"Wait for us, Robert, wait for us," she yelled.

But Robert was far into the distance in the direction of the planned rendezvous, with Scottie at his heel, and a bone in his mouth.

The clock on the tower began to buzz. Then, preceded by a timorous 'ping' and a 'pong' it began a series of thunderous, ear-splitting booms, alerting everyone, near and far, that midday had arrived. Everyone stopped what they were doing to put their hands over their ears. Katie counted out twelve nerve-shattering booms on Dottie's fingers to teach the child her numbers, then the pair continued on their way after Robert.

When Katie and Dottie arrived on the scene at MacTaggart's Landing, they saw that not only was the Major already there, with Mary and a photographer from *The Edinburgh Rocket,* but many of the townspeople had also gathered to witness the unusual event. Most were happy that their little village was to have a mention in a big city newspaper. Some were hoping to be seen in the photograph.

With the snow-covered mountain peaks in the distance, beautiful Loch Beiste spread majestically throughout the valley, with a light, silvery mist hovering on its surface, the little village looked pretty enough to be on the front of a Scottish calendar. The scene at MacTaggart's Landing, spoiled only by the sight of grumpy old Major Fordyce standing on a soap box, with his pistol-handled walking stick in one hand, a megaphone in the other, and the slavering Magnus at his feet. His only friend in the village, Marjory Meddle, in the front row of spectators looking on admiringly.

Fordyce had decided to use this opportunity to make his views about tourists, very clear to his fellow villagers. When he thought he had everyone's attention, the Major put the megaphone to his mouth.

"Now listen here, you people," he bellowed, in a dictatorial manner. "I hate tourists. I like my peace and quiet, and I don't care much who suffers financially!"

Pushing through the crowd to reach the front for a better view, Katie put her little sister down and cast her eyes around to find her brother. "I can't see Robert anywhere, can you, Dottie?"

Dottie found it difficult to answer because her mouth was so full of toffee. What came out sounded like a Martian from the planet Mars.

"And I wonder where Lachlan is? I noticed that his workshop was closed when we came by."

Dottie tried to reply, but could only speak Martian. "Mmmm, NNNNNmmmmm!"

"Quick, give me that bag of sweets, here comes Mum and Dad. We're supposed to be keeping them for Christmas." Katie confiscated the sweets just in the nick of time. "Hello Mum, hi, Dad," she smiled, hoping that the licorice hadn't blackened her teeth.

"Where's your brother got to?" Duncan asked, moving to the front of the crowd at MacTaggart's Landing where Fordyce stood.

"Shsssssssh," said a voice from behind them. It was the Reverend Brown. "Not that I agree with the wretched man, you understand, Laird, sir," he whispered. "I only want to hear what he has to say - so that I can argue with him later."

The Campbells nodded respectfully, and turned to listen to the Major's speech as little Dottie raised her arms to her father to be lifted up for a better view. He obliged, and they all stood together watching Fordyce lecture the villagers about the havoc tourists would create if they were encouraged to come to Airde.

With his soap box wavering precariously under foot as he became more animated, the Major ranted and raved, with the ends of his thick, curled moustache moving up and down at a furious pace as he spoke. He shouted and shrieked, his walking-stick poking angrily in the air as he made plain, his immeasurable dislike of invasive tourists.

Mary Sinclair, within ear-shot of the grumpy man, was busy taking notes, while her photographer was down on his haunches getting a close-up of Magnus and his thick, dribbling saliva.

Suddenly, while the Major was in full voice, from out of the shimmering lake behind him, there came the most tremendous, bloodcurdling, hair-raising, spine-tingling sound. Terrifying, ear-splitting roars were emanating from the silvery grey waters of the lake. The crowd of Airdians all gasped, and reached for their hearts.

Then they saw it. All eyes saw it. A thing. A monstrous thing! A thing that appeared right before their eyes, right behind Major Fordyce. Rising up out of the mist-covered water came a monstrous dragon head that spurted steam and a fountain of water skyward, like a geyser. Then they saw that the head sat upon a monstrously long neck, and a series of monstrous, bumpy humps.

"Aaaaaaaaaaaah!" Fordyce let out a yell that seemed to go on forever. His walking stick went one way, his megaphone the other, as he fell off his soapbox in shock, and landed on his backside in a puddle. Meanwhile, Magnus, his so called 'guard dog' went scampering away, yelping in fear, tail between his legs.

The monster, with a coat of shiny, slithery, serpenty-grey, glided through the water like a powerful torpedo. Then, with one last frightening roar, it dipped like a submarine, and disappeared into the shimmering waters of the lake.

In shock, the onlookers were galvanised to the spot on which they stood. No-one could believe what they'd seen.

"It's the dreaded Beastie!" cried one villager to break the silence.

"Aye. It's the Beast of Loch Beiste," said another.

Despite his fear, Stewart the newspaper photographer had managed to click his camera and take a photograph of the monster. His training had not let him down.

"Glory be," cried Reverend Brown.

"My Goodness me," cried Mrs McFee.

"And God Bless me," cried Molly McGhee.

"And Bless the Bones o' Prince Charlie," cried the Ghillie.

"Uncle 'Enry's Undies!" cried Underwood the Undertaker.

But, while all around, flabbergasted people reeled in shock, Mary Sinclair quickly gathered her wits about her. "Did you get a picture of the monster, Stewart?" she asked anxiously.

The crowd hushed to hear the answer, and all held their breath.

"Aye, I did that, Mary," he called back. "Aye, I did!"

"Well I can guarantee it'll be on the front page of tomorrow's *Edinburgh Rocket*," and the crowd cheered.

"That'll bring the tourists," Duncan Campbell remarked to his astonished wife.

"It will, won't it!" said young Robert, now standing beside him, with a grin from ear to ear. "I wonder how the Major will feel about that!"

The crowd began to laugh. At first with sniggers, then giggles, then building to all out raucous laughter, because they knew that once this news got out, all the world would want to visit Airde to see the monster for themselves. Contrary to Major Fordyce's loudly expressed desires.

Chapter 10

The assembled crowd were in no hurry to depart the scene at MacTaggart's Landing on this exciting Sunday morning, now only days away from Christmas. The appearance of the Loch Beiste Monster had given them much to talk about.

"Meet you back at the castle, Mum, Dad," said Robert to his parents, Lachlan said he would take me home."

"Oh, alright, Robert," said his father, not giving it another thought.

"Bye, Wobert," said Dottie, cradled in her father's arms.

"But don't be late for lunch," added Jean, as Robert walked quickly away.

Katie took it upon herself to chase after him, saying "I want to come too, Robert."

"No, Katie," he said, and he started to run off. "I've got something important to do."

"But I can do important things too, Robert. Let me come with you," she said, close to tears as she ran after him.

Robert stopped in his tracks and was about to be really angry with his sister, but he saw some of the villagers watching them, and he didn't want it to get back to his father that they were fighting in public. "Oh, alright, but don't make a fuss and draw attention to us, and only if you can keep a secret."

"You have an awful lot of secrets, Robert. What is it this time?"

Robert leaned in close to Katie and lowered his voice. "This, Katie Campbell, is probably the biggest secret you will ever have to keep, in all of your life! You have to cross your heart and promise that you'll keep it absolutely secret!" His face and his voice told her that he really, really meant it.

Katie put her hand to her heart and promised.

"Come on, then," he said reluctantly, with a frown, before hurrying off, Scottie leading the way, having hidden his bone for another day.

For nine full minutes they walked briskly, with Katie only just keeping up, and with Robert frequently looking back over his shoulder to make sure they weren't followed. Across a smooth grassy hill they went, and out of sight of the village, then down a bank, to a cove which was hidden behind trees, then on down toward the water's edge. To a secret place.

"This is where he launches it," Robert confided.

"Where who, launches what, Rob...?" she didn't complete the sentence. As they walked along the water's edge, her jaw dropped, just the way they say it does in books, when someone is suddenly astonished. Her eyes opened wide like saucers, just the way they say it does in books, when they are surprised, and she found it hard to put what she saw into words. She could only stammer. "The the, the, mmmmmmmmonster!" Her legs gave way, and she promptly sank down on her bottom, on the ground, in utter shock, while Robert hurried on, completely unafraid, to stand on rocks at the water's edge.

As they watched, the grey, slithery monster with the long neck and three humps, that the village had all seen earlier, came gliding silently into the shore.

While Katie sat stunned, legs outstretched in front of her, unable to move a muscle, a hatch in the top of the monster opened, and out popped the head and shoulders of Lachlan MacGregor, wearing his wet suit.

"Hello there, Robert. How was it, then?" he said, beaming.

"Absolutely terrific, Lachlan! You fooled everyone." He turned to Katie, "Come on, scardie-cat. It's not a real monster. Lachlan made it. But it looks real, doesn't it?"

Although Katie's heart was thumping inside her chest, she saw the funny side of it, and began to giggle, nervously. Her legs found their strength, she stood up, and ran to join Robert beside the water.

"You fooled the whole village, Lachlan," she stated, eyeing the 'monster.' And you fooled me, too. It's so real." She actually clapped her hands together in appreciation of his effort, but they made only a dull clap because she was wearing her mittens. But her enthusiasm and praise were enough to make Lachlan smile.

"Well now, Katie," Lachlan returned modestly, clambering out of the belly of the beast, and landing on the rocks. "I can't take all the credit. It was Robert's basic design."

"It's your best idea yet, Robert," she said. "I can see now why it had to be a secret."

"This will bring the tourists to Airde!" young Robert said confidently. "And..." he added cheekily, "I didn't actually PROMISE Dad that I wouldn't try something else!" He gave Katie an impish look. "Lachlan did all the hard work, and he built it in a day!"

"There's nothing like team-work, is there now," said the obliging Scotsman.

"How does it work, then Lachlan?" Katie asked.

"Why don't you jump inside and see for yourself, Katie? I'm just getting my breath back before I take it further down the loch to a spot I know, where no-one will ever find it."

And with that, he lifted Katie up and into the clever contraption.

The body of the mechanical monster which lay submerged beneath the surface of the water, was constructed from large, round drums, all welded together. Inside, there was a steering wheel, connected to a rudder at the back, and a bicycle seat, plus pedals and pullies attached, so Lachlan told Katie, to a set of paddles under the water which drove the monster forward and back, depending on which way the driver pedalled.

"Pedals, pullies, and paddles," Katie repeated, as she took it all in good-naturedly.

There were also little 'wings' under the water which Lachlan could tilt from the driver's seat to make the monster go under the water, or glide to the surface. The driver, meanwhile, breathed using an oxygen tank strapped on his back, or an aqualung as it's called. Its long neck had been made from black flexible plastic sewage pipe.

The outside coating, or the monster's 'skin' had been lined mostly with black bath-mats, smooth side down, prickly side up, and along the back, for effect, and looking very much like crocodile skin, Lachlan had made rubber shingles from pieces of old wellington boots, and glued and layered them on – the way a thatcher thatches a roof, then he painted them with dashes of slithery grey paint.

Katie was in awe. It was so big that she could stand up inside the body of the monster. And she couldn't resist reaching out to the steering wheel and all the operating levers as she sat on the driver's seat.

"What's this glass thing at eye level when I sit in the driver's seat, Lachlan?"

"It's a periscope, Katie," said Robert raising his eyebrows. "Don't girls know anything?" he said with a wink to Lachlan. "They use periscopes in submarines all the time."

"It's a braw bit of magic, that device, Katie," said Lachlan. "A wonderful invention. Just put your two hands on the handles and turn it, with your eyes to the little window, and you'll see 360 degrees all the way round. Front, sides, and all the way back to the front again. It's all done with mirrors, up through the monster's neck, and out its eyes. And you don't have to be on the surface to use it. You can see from under the water, while the monster is submerged."

Robert gave Lachlan a very proud grin.

"How did you decide what to make the monster's head look like, Lachlan?"

"I er, I modelled it on my old rocking horse. My mother has kept it all these years," he answered bashfully.

"How did you make the monstrous roars? Those sounds were scary."

"There's a mouthpiece beside the periscope there. It's from my grandfather's trumpet. I knew he wouldn't mind. He was a bit of a prankster himself, you know. I 'borrowed' it, and connected it to a speaker, a microphone, and my sound system – the bell of his euphonium makes a fantastic deep boom. I made all that loud and scary noise myself." He grinned, adding, "My mother always called me her 'wee monster.'"

"And what about the water-spout? That was fantastic!" said Katie, looking over the humps for a tell-tale sign.

"Oh, that? Well, that's all done with a pump I borrowed from my mother's garden fountain. She can't use it in this weather because the little stream of water freezes too quickly. The mechanism sucks in water from the loch, into that cooker you see, run by gas, and it sucks, cooks, pumps, and shoots. It's perfect for a steamy water spout."

"Great, isn't it, Katie?" Robert enthused. "This has got to be the most difficult secret you've ever had to keep."

"It sure is," Katie agreed, as Lachlan lifted her out of the monster and set her back on dry land. "But it's fantastic!"

"I was thinking, for the next run," Lachlan began, "that I might use my motorbike battery to give the monster flashing red eyes. What do you think, kids?"

"WOW!" they said in unison. Scottie barked.

Chapter 11

The Edinburgh Rocket sold out next morning. It had never had a headline like this one before: 'LOCH BEISTE HAS MONSTER!' It was splashed in huge letters right across the front page, and beneath it, a photograph of the monster in the lake, with Major Fordyce falling off his soapbox with a look of horror on his ugly face.

Across Scotland, in every home, people of every age put aside their manners to read the paper at the breakfast table. And in the village of Airde, in houses, in shops, and in the street, The Airdians peered over shoulders to read about their very own Loch Beiste Monster.

Meanwhile, the editor of *The Inverness Flyer* was displeased by this turn of events. The district of Inverness had much to lose in this monstrous affair, so *The Inverness Flyer* had its own bold headline, showing its displeasure, when it defiantly printed 'NESSIE KIDNAPPED' on its front page. This was accompanied by a three-page article, suggesting that a tunnel went underground from Loch Ness to Loch Beiste, and somehow, mysteriously, their beloved Nessie had found her way to Loch Beiste. Or, worse still, it had been lured there by the unscrupulous Airdians.

At Castle Airde that morning, Robert Campbell and Scottie were first out of bed. First to scamper down the stairs. First to run to the front door to fetch the newspaper, and Robert was first to read about their very own, clever, secretive handiwork. Handiwork that he and Lachlan had mischievously concocted together. He raced with Scottie through to the warmth of the kitchen, *The Edinburgh Rocket* in hand. He threw two logs onto the embers of the fire, but he could not contain his excitement long enough, to sit down and read the whole article written by Mary Sinclair. Instead, he rang his friend and collaborator before anyone else in the castle could overhear.

"Lachlan, have you seen the Edinburgh paper?" he whispered excitedly down the phone line. "We did it! We did it! We fooled them, we fooled them all, Lachlan!"

"Aye, that we did, laddie," Lachlan chuckled, "Haven't had so much fun in years."

"When can we do it again?"

"Again? Well now Robert," he began. "I am mighty pleased that it went so well, I must admit. And it did my heart good to see that old grump Fordyce fall of his soap box." He found it difficult to hold back a chuckle at the memory. "Our poor wee village could certainly do with an injection of funds at the moment."

"So? When can we show the monster again?"

"My dear mother always says that you shouldn't overdo a good thing. Besides, every time we show the monster, it increases the risk of our scheme being discovered. We have to be careful lad." he cautioned.

"Just once more before Christmas Lachlan. Please?"

"How about we wait and see what the reaction to the story is, before we make any plans? That sounds reasonable, doesn't it?"

"Oh, alright," said Robert showing his disappointment. "That does sound reasonable, I suppose."

"Cheer up, Robert. It's my bet that news teams will start arriving from all over the place today. I'm making Bed and Breakfast signs for the Ghillie and others in the village in readiness. I'll nail one up at the castle junction later. So tell your mother to prepare for callers. We'll have a good Christmas out of this yet, you wait and see!"

"But what about the Major? He's not going to like this. He might try to stop people coming into Airde."

"Tell you what I'll do, young Robert, why don't you and I meet at the Major's gate at ten o'clock this morning. We'll make sure he doesn't get up to any tricks."

"Really? You mean it, Lachlan?"

"A good Scotsman never says anything he doesn't mean. You should know that by now, Robert."

"And you're a good Scotsman, Lachlan."

"And you're a good lad, Robert Campbell. By the way, did you see what Mary Sinclair has called our monster?"

"No."

"Well, she's called it 'Lady.' 'The Lady of The Lake.'"

"Huh! Typical thing for a girl to do."

"You do realise that Loch Beiste actually means 'Lake of The Beast?' He gave Robert a moment to think about this, then said, "I must away now, Robert, I'll be seeing you at ten o'clock at Fordyce's gate."

"I'll be there, Lachlan. I'll be there."

#

Lachlan proved to be right. It was the beginning of a siege on Airde by sight-seeing tourists and the media. People were arriving from all over the place.

"Good morning, Lachlan," said Mary Sinclair, who was already on the scene with Stewart her photographer, on the outskirts of the village, near Fordyce's gate, when Lachlan, Robert and Scottie arrived. "Great minds think alike, then?" she smiled.

Grinning, Lachlan was quick to answer. "There's never been any doubt about your quick wit, Mary Sinclair."

Robert couldn't help but notice the warm looks the pair exchanged.

Suddenly they heard the sound of a tractor engine, and turning around, they saw Major Fordyce driving through his gate on his biggest tractor, towing a long, six-wheeled trailer with the dribbling Magnus riding on it, like a potentate of ancient Rome. And, as they all watched in amazement, the Major parked tractor and trailer right across the road, blocking it completely. Then he stopped the engine, took out the ignition key, and hopped down to the ground with a satisfied look on his face. "That'll stop any tourists in their tracks," he declared.

"You can't do that, Major," shouted Lachlan.

"I can! And I have!" Fordyce yelled back smugly, as he strode back toward his property, leaving Magnus in the trailer like a soldier on guard. He stood behind his gate, arms folded defiantly.

But before they could exchange another word, a state-of-the-art coach rolled up, (the latest design, and very expensive) full of Japanese tourists, heading for the village, to see the monster for themselves. The driver, Jock MacLavender, a caber-tossing Highlander, a goliath of a man, who wore tartan trousers and a matching tam-o'-shanter, (the traditional Scottish cap with a tassle), got out, and marched toward them all. "What's the meaning of this?" he demanded to know.

"What's it look like?" answered Fordyce. "Road's blocked. You'll have to turn back."

Jock glowered, then marched angrily back to his bus and blasted his horn, again and again, causing an almighty din, and every little Japanese head on either side of the coach popped out of its window, to see what the fuss was all about.

"That'll do you no good," said the Major. "I'm not budging!"

"Let my coach pass," yelled Jock, leaning out of his driver's window, "or I'll push yer silly wee tractor aside with my coach."

"You do, and I'll have the police onto you!" said Fordyce, with Magnus backing him up by growling at the driver, showing his canines, saliva dripping, drooling and dribbling, and with that evil look in his eye, head tucked in, and ready to pounce.

"If you DON'T let me pass, I'll have the police onto YOU!" Jock countered. "And ye' can shut that mutt up - or I'll bite his tail."

They exchanged insults for a time, with Mary Sinclair taking notes, and her photographer snapping pictures of the angry stand-off. Full credit to Jock for keeping his temper in check, for the mighty driver could so easily have tossed the aggressive Major Fordyce like a caber, but common sense prevailed.

It took over an hour for a police car to come down from Edinburgh, siren wailing, and when it sloughed to a halt at the sizzling scene of the confrontation, all four doors of the Rover opened at once. Three young Scottish constables, and the burly Detective Sergeant Donald MacDonald stepped out. In full view of tourists, the media, Mary, the photographer, Lachlan, and a young lad who was trying very hard not to giggle with the excitement of it all.

The Major received a jolly good scolding from an angry Detective Sergeant MacDonald for being so selfish and disagreeable, and making him travel all the way from Edinburgh. He made Major Fordyce remove his tractor from the road, warning him not to obstruct it again. Scottie barked his approval.

Turning to Lachlan, and whispering in his ear, the very bonnie Mary Sinclair asked a question, which proved how very astute she was. "Tell me, Lachlan," she said, her blue eyes alight with mischief, "do you think there might be another day when the monster might be going by? I'd hate to miss it."

A grin stretched across Lachlan's manly face. "Well, now Mary, being a very proper, 'Lady of The Lake,' I'd imagine she'd wait till after Church on Sunday to take another leisurely swim. That way," he added, "the newspapers will still have plenty of time to tell the world by Monday morning." He gave a cheeky wink. "Mind you, Mary, I'm only guessing."

#

Over the next few days an invasion of media people came from all over the country, and as expected, from places as far away as Tasmania, Timbuktu, and Trinidad and Tobago, to converge on the village. Journalists, photographers, and television crews, as well as busloads of tourists - all began arriving in a steady stream.

Every roll of film in the village, sold within the first few days. The Post Office sold out of post cards and stamps, and food and produce of every kind had to be brought in to replenish supplies. The coffee shop began selling tea – and the tea room had to sell coffee. But the cash registers rang gaily, non-stop, and bulged with cash. And the villagers all had smiles on their faces.

As for the farmers, the lights in their hen-houses burned all night, so that the hens would lay more eggs to meet demand, and lights were erected around the paddocks so the cows would produce more milk. Neither man nor beast, was exempt from longer hours and harder work, during this time. Like little squirrels, the Airdians worked assiduously while there was plenty, to hoard their little bit extra, for a rainy day.

From time to time, sneaky old Fordyce hid behind a tree beside his gate glowering at this daily influx of visitors. Then he hit upon an idea. He and Meddle set up a tent outside his gate, with snarling Magnus at their side, and charged a toll of everyone who passed.

It cost a hundred Scottish pounds for every coach. Fifty pounds per car. Twenty-five pounds for a motorbike. Ten pounds for a bicycle, and one pound per person on foot. Some people refused to pay, and were turned away, but the majority paid up, hoping to see the monster. The cagey old hypocrite, Fordyce, pocketed two thousand, one hundred and fifty two pounds on that very first day.

When the villagers came to hear of this unofficial toll gate, they sent for the police again. The Major quickly ceased charging after that, but he had signalled that he was prepared to do just about anything, to prevent Airde from becoming a Mecca for invading foreigners.

#

"If this keeps up, Duncan," said Jean Campbell to her husband up at Castle Airde, as she turned off her bedside lamp, after another exhausting day spent cooking, and cleaning up behind her paying guests, "We may not have to sell the castle after all."

"It will take a lot more than a few Bed and Breakfasts to solve our financial troubles, Jean," Duncan Campbell wearily sighed.

"But Duncan, we mustn't spoil the children's Christmas."

"No. I would never spoil their Christmas. We won't talk about having to sell Castle Airde in front of the children. Goodnight, dear."

"Goodnight dear," she replied resolutely.

Chapter 12

Ding-Dong. Ding-Dong, the bells did chime. They resounded triumphantly in the glens, across the lake, and they echoed throughout the mountains, in a joyous, melodious medley to celebrate the season. It was Christmas Eve.

The little village of Airde dressed in its pristine, white winter coat, looked like a painted picture as snow-flakes fell gently down, and the church-bells peeled for the third time that Sunday morning. At nine o-clock they had sounded a wake-up call to the villagers. At eleven o-clock they had welcome them to church, and now, at Midday, they were announcing that the special Christmas church service was over.

Five elderly male bell ringers in bright red garb, with rose-red cheeks, vigorously tugged at the great twine ropes attached to the ancient bells. These gallant souls had played their Christmas tunes on each and every anniversary of Christmas since they were boys.

The great double-doors of the church sprang open, and Scottie was amongst the first to run out into the crisp outside air, followed by Robert, then Katie, while their parents shook hands with a smiling Reverend Brown, and wished him a merry Christmas. A happy man was the reverend, for the church's coffers had been filled to overflowing with coins this day. Thanks to the visiting tourists, the purses of the Airdians were full.

"See you at the children's Christmas party this afternoon, Laird," said the cake-loving reverend. "I'm looking forward to tasting your Australian lamingtons, Mrs Campbell," he said, licking his lips.

"And wait till you try my pavlova, Reverend, I won the Aussie Bake-Off three years in a row with my pavlovas," Jean proudly said, shaking the religious man's hand as they passed through the church door.

Just then, Duncan Campbell spotted Robert running off at an alarming rate through the milling congregation "Where are you off to, Robert?" he shouted.

"To see the monster," came his reply, as Scottie barked in agreement, running by his side.

"He HOPES to see the monster!" Katie corrected, trying to keep the secret, as she raced off after him, leaving Dottie with her parents.

Just then, there came a bone-chilling, thunderous roar from the lake near MacTaggart's Landing. It was a roar so loud that the mighty bells in the tower jingled of their own accord. The thing – that monstrous thing – that mighty, roaring thing – had returned!

The Campbells, Duncan and Jean, looked to one another as the whole congregation fled the church and headed in the direction of the Village Green overlooking MacTaggart's Landing where they could see the lake. For there, a handful of journalists and cameramen, Mary Sinclair among them, were getting the scoop of their lives. The Campbells, along with Scottie, all hurried to join the sea of children and adults who now flocked to see the monster. Some, for the first time.

At this moment, the light snowfall ebbed away, and the clouds parted, allowing rays of sunshine to peek through from the sky, as the monster made its way far out into the middle of the lake. Dipping and plunging. Bobbing and ducking.

Even from the distance, its mighty roar seemed to rock the village. With every eye upon it, the monster began sprouting water like a whale; a mighty vortex of water sprouted from it, shot into the air, then fell in an umbrella-shaped spray, while hissing steam gushed from its nostrils.

The crowd gasped in astonishment. They huddled together in awe, they whispered in wonder, they jumped up and down, they pointed, they giggled, they chortled. Children squealed at the sight, some in fear, some with glee. And young Robert Campbell grinned from ear to ear, and gave Scottie a big cuddle.

"Someone get a boat," called Molly McGhee. We might be able to catch it!"

"Och, let it be," called the Ghillie. "We dinna want to fright it!"

But even as he spoke, its mighty head dove down into the icy lake, then, first one hump disappeared, then two, then three humps disappeared from sight, and with a happy wiggle of its tail, it slipped beneath the water and was gone for another day.

"Hurray," shouted the crowd. "Hurray, for The Lady of the Lake. She brings us good fortune for Christmas."

"And a full belly," cried one robust Airdian patting his well-filled stomach.

"Did you get photographs?" Mary Campbell called out to Stewart her photographer, above the noisy crowd. All heads turned in his direction.

"Aye, that I did, Mary!" He nodded, and with a great grin on his cheery face, he held up his old Hasselblad camera, and the crowd cheered.

"Let's hurry then, and I'll get the film back to Edinburgh," she said with a smile. And, as Mary watched on, her photographer rewound the film, took it out from his camera and handed it to her. She thought wryly to herself, 'I never thought I would find a reason to be calling Lachlan MacGregor 'a monster,' but he surely is a fine one.' You see, Mary had worked out the secret behind the monster of Loch Beiste – but she was keeping that secret to herself.

As she turned to go on her way, she bumped straight into the Campbells.

"You'll have some clear shots of The Lady this morning, Mary," said Duncan.

"Oh, hello Mr Campbell, Laird, sir, Mrs Campbell." She smiled coyly with great respect for the popular couple from Australia. "Merry Christmas to you all. Yes, it's a beautiful morning for taking photographs. What a spectacle!"

Suddenly, Little Dottie jerked away from her father's clutches, and held her arms out for Mary to take her. "Mary, Mary," she cried, and leaned over to the pretty journalist to carry her.

Mary took Dottie and gave her a motherly cuddle, the way that loving women do with young children, while the Campbell family looked on approvingly. Everyone liked Mary Sinclair.

"Will you be at the Children's Christmas party this afternoon, Mary?" asked Jean.

"Yes. The paper wants me to do a story on it. But right now, I'm on my way to make sure this morning's photographs are sent to Edinburgh. My photographer has another assignment to go to, so I'm arranging to send the film off, you see."

She went to give little Dottie back to her father Duncan, but the child protested vehemently. "Oh, dearie me, Mrs Campbell, I'm sorry. The bairn seems to have taken a shine to me today."

She tried a second time to give Dottie back to her parents, but no, little Dottie had made her own mind up. She wanted to stay with Mary a while longer. "Well in that case," Mary declared, "why don't I take the three of you with me for a ride to the bus depot on the main road, then drop you back at the Christmas Party later?"

The girls were happy about this, but the look on Robert's face showed that he was none too keen. He had other plans – he wanted to visit Lachlan, but his parents insisted he go along too, to keep an eye on the girls. When Mary announced that Scottie was also welcome, he agreed.

"Come on then, let's go," enthused Mary. "There's room enough in the van for all of us, and there's some warm pastries in there that the baker gave me just a few minutes ago. They'll keep us going until the party," she smiled.

Are you sure you can handle them all, Mary?" asked Jean Campbell.

"Aye! It'll be fun. And it'll give you time to wrap their Christmas presents without them spying on you, Mrs Campbell," she laughed, marching off with Dottie cuddling into her shoulder, and sucking her thumb. And off they went, Katie on one side, Robert the other, and Scottie leading the way to the van.

With a quickly scribbled note to the editor of the newspaper, to let him know what was in the package - the latest story and photographs of the monster, together with a Christmas card, a Walker's tartan tin full of pure butter shortbread, and a Dundee Cake - they set off to deliver the package to the depot, where it would be collected by the next bus travelling through to Edinburgh.

Chapter 13

It was a pleasant journey filled with cheery talk, for there was much to discuss. Robert was interested to know what it meant to be a journalist, and asked Mary what she did the rest of the time, if she only worked on special assignments for *The Edinburgh Rocket*. Mary went on to explain that she was presently studying Scottish History, and hoped to be Scotland's first lady Prime Minister.

"Wow!" said the children.

"Woof" Scottie commented.

The depot was a place which old David Dunbar called home. His living quarters were at the rear of the building, with a grand walled garden, and the despatch office, with its long oak receiving desk, was at the front. The children alighted from Mary's van to meet and greet him, and wish him well for Christmas. Mary left the package for dispatch, then they all waved him goodbye as they happily set off, back to the village in Mary's little white van.

Travelling along, with eyes glued to the road ahead, Robert's attention was drawn to a vehicle he recognised. "Stop!" he yelled. "That's Marjory Meddle's yellow Morgan turning in there." He pointed to a shady nook off the highway. His little heart thumping fast now. It was a very important location, for Robert knew that this was the place where Lachlan hid the monster.

Mary slowed the van to watch the oncoming automobile with interest. Then, just as she pulled over to the side, and stopped her engine, a white van, very much like her own, came zooming out from the inlet at an alarming rate. The name along its side read: *The Inverness Flyer.*

"I wonder what's going on!" she said in almost a whisper, her mind ticking over like a super-sleuth, as she watched the van speed past them, heading back along the main road.

"I think I know, said Robert," with a worried look on his face. "I think they're spying on Lachlan. That's where he keeps the..." He suddenly clammed up, not wanting to reveal the secret of the monster.

Mary's head spun around to look at him. The mere mention of Lachlan's name took Mary's interest. "You don't mean to tell me that this might have something to do with the monster, do you, Robert?"

"Well, er, em... oh, I don't want to say, Mary."

"It's alright, Robert. I know about Lachlan's man-made monster. I guessed a while back."

Katie gasped. "Oh, dearie, dearie me," she said, not realising how much she sounded like the locals, from time to time now. "Oh, dear, I hope he doesn't get into any trouble."

"So do I, Katie, so do I," said Mary. "He did it with the best of intentions. There's no doubt about that. And we can't let him get into trouble for it. The Major would have a field day, if he were to find out the secret." She sat thinking about what to do for a moment, then as any curious reporter would, she decided she just couldn't sit back and watch the Major and Marjory Meddle blow the whistle on Lachlan. "I'm going to see what they're up to. You three wait here," she said as she opened the van door.

"NO!" they protested together.

"We want see too," Dottie cried. Her comment was followed by a sharp 'Woof' from Scottie.

"I did invent the monster after all," boasted Robert proudly.

"And I kept it a secret," Katie added, equally proudly.

"Oh, alright then," Mary conceded. "But we must be very careful. And very quiet. You stay here Scottie and mind the van."

Scottie whined sadly at being left behind, but did as he was instructed. He watched as they climbed the sloping embankment which looked down on the inlet on the other side to get a better view.

On the rise of the slippery bank, Mary let out a muffled gasp, and abruptly came to a halt. She turned to the children, and put a finger up to her lips for absolute quiet. For there, almost directly beneath them, was not only Marjory Meddle's Morgan, but Fordyce's Land Rover, and a third vehicle, a big, grubby, uncared for lorry, which sat hidden, further away beneath the trees.

Its occupants, three of the most scurrilous looking men Mary had ever seen, were climbing down from the back of the truck. Laughing amongst themselves, after bundling something inside, they walked towards Fordyce and Meddle.

Mary, worried about Lachlan now, felt a sick feeling in her tummy, and decided that these criminal types were up to some serious mischief, but she was not sure what. Should she try and climb down further, closer, nearer to the danger, to see if she could overhear their conversation? Or, should she stay back and not risk being spotted?

Her curiosity got the better of her. What was the meaning of this secretive meeting in this hidden nook off the main road? What on earth was going on with this weird mix of people? Mary wanted very much to know. "I'm going to move a little closer to try and hear what the Major is plotting."

But Katie grasped her arm. "No, Mary. Don't go any further, please. It's much too dangerous. Please don't go."

Mary smiled at Katie to reassure her. "It's alright, sweetheart. I'll be careful, I promise. But you must all stay put – those truckies look mighty dangerous to my mind."

Leaving the children hiding behind a boulder, she moved forward, slowly, stealthily. Never wanting to be beaten by any situation that presented itself to her, she bravely closed in on the gathering. But suddenly, without warning, she slipped on the slimy wet ground beneath her feet, and went tumbling down the grassy hillside – right into the arms of one of the truckies.

"Oh, no!' cried Robert. "I'm going down after her. Stay there, Katie."

"No, Robert! You can't. They'll get you too! Please don't go. Don't leave us here!" Katie pleaded, looking down at Dottie's worried face as the youngster clung tight to her hand.

"I've got to, Katie!" And before she could protest any further, Robert was off down the slope to rescue Mary, shouting furiously at the men. "Leave her alone. Let her go, you Neanderthals!" It was a new word he'd learned only the week before, when studying human evolution.

"Or you'll what?" shouted one of the gang, laughing, thinking it incredulous that someone as young as Robert, could be so bold as to want to tackle them. But with all eyes upon him, Robert came hurtling down the hillside, his legs going faster than they ever had before. So fast in fact, that sadly, he too lost control of them, and tumbled over. Head over heels he went. Over, and over, and over again, until he too, landed right at the feet of the truckie gang. And there he sat, stunned and embarrassed while the scruffy men all laughed at him.

Katie glanced down at Dottie with a look of anguish on her face. "Oh dearie me," she said, "now what do we do, Dottie?"

"Scottie!" was her reply.

Katie's eyes lit up. "Yes! Of course! Good girl. Why didn't I think of that! He might be able to frighten those men, and give Robert and Mary a chance to escape. Come on, let's go back to the van and let him out." And she held tight to her little sister's hand and guided her carefully back down the hillside toward the road, then they ran as fast as their little legs would permit, back to Mary's van. At the roadside, Katie opened the van door to allow Scottie to jump out.

The intelligent collie took a giant leap out of the van and onto the roadway, speeding away like a bullet train. He instinctively knew what he had to do. He raced in the direction of the inlet, where he sensed that Robert was in deep trouble, without as much as a word from Katie.

He ran and ran, and very soon he was there, hovering behind a rock, able to take in the whole scene in an instant. Mary had her hands tied behind her back, and was being led toward the truck by one of the truckies, while another was about to tie Robert up. Scottie knew that if Robert was taken into the truck, like Mary was, the baddies could close the tailgate on him, and he too could be trapped, with no way that Scottie could save him.

Scottie crept up on them, on his belly, crawling silently. Then, down in the gully, he sprang forward with a mighty leap, up into the face of one of the ugly truckies, who soon let go of Robert, despite his tight grip. Seeing this, another of the truckies moved to grab hold of Robert so that he could tie him up, but Robert struggled against him. Scottie then took his chance. He pounced, and gave the ugly brute a sharp bite on the nose.

With a pained cry the man quickly let go of Robert and fell to the ground. Scottie yapped sharply at the third man, who now backed away fearfully.

Then Scottie grabbed at the back of Robert's jacket, suggesting he make his getaway quickly, and Robert was quick to take his advice. He ran off as fast as his young legs would carry him, with Scottie fighting a rear-guard action, warding off the three men with fierce growls and snapping teeth, giving Robert the best chance of escape.

Panting, Robert reached Mary's van and his waiting, worried sisters. "We'll have to hide," said Robert, out of breath. "We can't stay with the van. They could break the windows and get at us. Come on, quickly, in here, in the bushes!" He bent and scooped up little Dottie, and ran with her in his arms, while Katie hurried along at his heel, into a dense thicket of bushes.

"Thank goodness for Scottie," said Katie.

"A genuine 'wonder dog', declared Robert.

"Fank you Scottie, said Dottie sweetly, to her absent friend.

"But what's going to happen to Mary?" Katie blurted, close to tears.

"And what's happened to Lachlan, and the monster?" said Robert, equally worried "And what are Major Fordyce and Marjory Meddle up to?"

They waited. Alone and afraid. Then suddenly they saw Scottie streak past them at a speed of knots.

"Why's he leaving us here?" said Robert, half to himself.

They hunched low. Afraid. It was all so quiet. No birds were singing. Not a living thing made a noise.

"I'm scared," Kate admitted. "I hope there are no wolves, here, especially now that we don't have Scottie for protection."

Robert put his forefinger up to his lips to warn them they should be quiet. He didn't want to say it out loud, but agreed whole-heartedly about the wolves. The three youngsters cuddled together likes babes in the woods, to comfort each other, as dark clouds rolled in.

Dottie began to sing very quietly to herself. She always sang when she was afraid. "The inky, winky spider..."

"Shhhhhhh! Be quiet, Dottie," said Robert. Then, after anxious moments amidst the uneasy silence, Robert thought he could hear something rustling in the bushes. With heart pounding, he told his sisters to be still. He made them listen. "Shhhhhhh!" he whispered, putting his forefinger up to his lips again. "Something's moving in the bushes over there."

The hairs on Robert's arms stood up. A quiver ran down his spine. They all heard the sound of heavy breathing. Then, they saw two brown eyes peep through the bushes only feet away. The three held their breath...

"Scottie!" Dottie exclaimed, as a familiar wet nose poked into view.

"You clever dog," said Robert, patting him victoriously, with Katie joining in. "You fooled them."

Stealthily, like a trained sheep dog, he crawled on his belly through the thicket toward them, panting. Dottie wrapped her arms around his neck as he licked her face in greeting.

"Did you see what they've done with Mary?" Robert asked his canine companion. "And what's happened to Lachlan?" He quizzed his canine friend. "Oh, how I wish you could talk, Scottie."

Chapter 14

"I'm worried, Duncan, said Jean. The children's Christmas party is about to start, and there's no sign of the children, or Mary Sinclair! What on earth could have happened to them?" Jean stood behind their empty seats at the long, trestle-table in the Village Hall, with scores of babbling children nearby, drowning out her troubled words.

Duncan stood shaking his head. "Beats me, Jean. This is not like Mary at all. She's always reliable. I'll give her another five minutes, then I'll go looking for them."

"Why wait, Duncan. Please go now. I'm really worried. They might have had an accident in Mary's van."

"Now don't you go getting yourself all worked up, Jean Campbell, I'll find them,"

After kissing his wife tenderly on the cheek, Duncan hurried out to his car, an elderly, and slightly battered Jaguar, which his youngsters had named Jeremy.

After driving around and around the village in Jeremy Jaguar, in a vain search for his children, he set off along the road to the highway, towards the depot - Mary's destination when she'd set off with the children in tow.

Turning from the village road to traverse the highway, Duncan could not believe what his eyes were seeing. Scottie was running toward his car, barking furiously, with Robert chasing after him; Katie and little Dottie were straggling along well behind them, holding hands. And they all looked very distressed.

"What happened?" Duncan asked, when he pulled up and opened the car door for them. "Are you alright? Where's

Mary?" Has there been an accident?" As the questions gushed out of Duncan, Scottie bounded into the car, and over to the back seat.

"We...She...They..." Out of breath, Robert tried to answer, but his words tumbled out all jumbled up, amid gasps for air, so that his father had to tell him to stop, and catch his breath first, so that he could make some sense of it all.

Duncan grabbed up his two girls, both now in tears, and gave each one a hug. "Now, now, now," said Duncan, trying to pacify his lovely daughters. "Whatever it is that's happened, it's not the end of the world. I'm sure we can fix it."

"Bad men," Dottie panted.

"They've got Mary," Katie added.

"Who have?" Duncan scowled.

"The men with the lorry, Dad," said Robert, now that he'd caught his breath. "They've kidnapped Mary!"

"Come on now..." Duncan said sceptically. "What men? What lorry?"

"It's true, Dad," Katie concurred, wiping away a tear. They were horrible, ugly men, and they've kidnapped Mary."

"Ugwy men," declared Dottie, lowering her chin, turning down her lips, screwing up her eyes, pulling her eyebrows together, and making a very unpleasant face indeed. "Hobble men."

"Ooooh, yeeees?" said Duncan, obviously very suspicious about their fanciful story. "Show me where you last saw Mary." He started up the engine, and followed the youngsters' directions. "I'd like to know just what the devil has been going on!" He sounded very displeased indeed.

And what parent wouldn't be distressed when he saw his children running along a highway, all alone.

So Robert told the story in a very grown-up, methodical way. Slowly, from the beginning, with Katie adding extra bits for effect. All about the Major and Marjory Meddle's car, and the van from *The Inverness Flyer,* and the truck with the three nasty truckies. And then Mary slipping down the embankment, and getting caught, then Robert getting caught, then how Scottie helped Robert escape their clutches. But, he did not give away their secret – about Lachlan and his fake monster – which left a great big gap in the story, which only added to Duncan's suspicions about their story.

Then, when they reached the place on the roadway where Mary had left her van, it was nowhere to be seen. So they drove on into the inlet, to where the big lorry had been. But there was nothing to be seen there either. Not a car. Not a truck. And certainly no sign of Mary Sinclair.

The Campbells all got out of the car and each one of the children, singularly, and together, shouted out Mary's name. And Scottie barked. They shouted non-stop, in an effort to attract Mary's attention – if she was still in the area.

Duncan scratched his head. "I find it very hard to believe your story, children. Is this another one of your inventions? Like the Castle Airde Ghost Tours?"

"NO!" they chorused, realising that their story was not going to be believed.

"Well, I think it is. And you've got Mary Sinclair to play along with you. I'll have to have a word with her about this. Come on, you're late for the Christmas party. Although you really don't deserve to go to a party for worrying your mother."

"But it's all true, Dad. Look, tyre marks. Four different sets, Major Fordyce, Marjory Meddle, *The Inverness Flyer*, plus the big trucks. Just like we told you." Then he ran off around the point to where Lachlan normally kept the monster. A moment later he let out an unholy yelp. "Oh, NO!" he yelled. "They've got the monster too, Dad. The kidnappers have taken our monster too!" He stood frozen to the spot, his face deathly pale as he looked at the pile of canvas which Lachlan had used to cover the monster when it wasn't in use.

Katie ran to join her brother, then turned back to her father. "Yes, they've taken the monster, too, Dad. Lachlan's fake monster."

When Duncan Campbell, carrying little Dottie, followed Katie's footsteps and saw the empty hideout for himself, he stood shaking his head in disbelief. "I've got to admit this is more original than the ghost tours," he said with a wry grin. "Kidnapping a fake monster." He looked into the eyes of his children. "But I'm not fooled about the kidnapping, kids. Come on, the party's waiting for us back at the village. And as you're the children of the Laird, you have to attend."

"But Dad?" Robert and Katie protested together.

Duncan had run out of patience with them. "Enough of this nonsense. Not another word about monsters and kidnappers. Back in the car. Now!"

Chapter 15

Christmas crackers popped like fireworks, multi-coloured balloons hung like grapes, streamers zoomed like shooting stars, whistles whistled, and trumpets blew. There was laughter and giggles as Santa gave gifts, and it was noisy as a zoo. Pork pies, pavlovas, and parfaits galore, hundreds and thousands - the first to go. Chocolate crackle crunchies, all gobbled with glee. Chocolate-chip Clown Cake munched with delight. Marshmallow Snowmen all yummy and white, with ice-cream and jelly in every bite.

But the Campbell children were in no mood to enjoy the party while their minds were on Mary Sinclair and the monster. Even Scottie lay listless in a far corner, his head lowered between his paws, watching the partying crowd with sad eyes.

And well they might be worried, for the monster, which had brought the village such jubilation only hours before, now lay in a crumpled heap in the dirty old truck which was hidden in Major Fordyce's barn. And, Mary and Lachlan both, lay tightly bound in a cold dark cellar beneath the barn, with the fierce Magnus standing guard over the trap door.

This is what happened...

After a successful outing on the lake, Lachlan had taken the monster to its secret hiding place, the little inlet in the sheltered bay, where it would remain safe until needed again. He had not noticed *The Inverness Flyer* newspaperman hiding in the bushes, nor heard the click of his camera. Nor did he notice the furtive little man hurrying away with secret photographs – photographs of Lachlan climbing out of the belly of the man-made beast.

Feeling very satisfied with his handiwork, Lachlan, having completed the task of hiding the monster with a tarpaulin and bracken, began to strip off his tight, black, rubber, wet-suit, unaware that he was being watched by spies and intruders. And, half way through disrobing, whilst his arms were held tight by the constricting rubber garment, the three brawny truckies hired by Major Fordyce, Boris, Thumper, and Dingbat, had overpowered him.

They knew that only at this most vulnerable of moments, with his arms locked inside his underwater wet-suit as he tried to remove it, could the mighty Lachlan be overpowered. And it would take no less than three men to do it! The Major had then instructed his henchmen to bind Lachlan up and bundle him into the truck. It was at this time that Mary Sinclair had stumbled down the embankment, straight into the arms of the truckies, so she too was tied and thrown into the truck, not knowing that her dear friend Lachlan was already held captive inside. But the truckies hadn't been so lucky with young Robert – Scottie had come to his rescue.

Watched with self-satisfied grins on the faces of Fordyce and Meddle, as instructed, the three mean-spirited truckies had proceeded to break up the monster. They tore at it, and broke it apart, into pieces small enough to fit into their vehicle, and threw it in beside their two prisoners. Then they drove off, laughing at what they had done, followed by Major Fordyce and Marjory Meddle in their own vehicles, who were excited at the prospect of revealing to the world, that the Loch Beiste Monster was nothing but a hoax.

"Lachlan!" Mary had cried out in astonishment as she was thrown into the truck. "They've got you too, then?"

Lachlan was feeling more than a little embarrassed about being tied up like a kipper on Hogmanay, and not being able to save Mary from this humiliation. "I'm sorry that you had to be mixed up in this travesty, Mary," he said, like the gentleman he was.

"What do you think is going to happen to us, Lachlan?"

"I wish I knew, Mary. I wish I knew."

#

It was growing dark when the old Ford truck came to a halt outside Fordyce's shed. Mary and Lachlan were bundled out, leaving the dismembered, very sad-looking monster behind. Then they were ushered into Fordyce's barn. With the only light a small lantern, and no heating, the pair were pushed carelessly through a trap-door, down steps, and into the icy cold cellar beneath the barn, tied to a pillar, and warned not to cause trouble, or try to escape.

Fordyce stood at the top of the steps looking down at his prey with a look of intense pleasure on his normally grumpy face, as if he'd just won the Grand Lottery. "Well, well, well," he smirked, arms folded across his chest and resting atop his fat belly. "Got yourselves all tied up, have you? That'll teach you to poke your noses in where they don't belong. Won't it now?"

"You won't get away with this Fordyce," Lachlan blasted back. "Whatever it is that you're up to, there's no need to dish up this kind of treatment to a lady like Mary Sinclair. You should be ashamed of yourself."

"Drastic situations require drastic measures old boy," Fordyce retorted. "But don't worry, you'll be freed again. But not 'till I'm good and ready!" he warned.

"And when might that be?" Mary asked with a fighting spirit.

"When your opposition newspaper *The Inverness Flyer* has shed a little light on this outrageous duplicity, this fraudulent deceit, this diabolical double-dealing, this demonic deception, which you have wantonly perpetrated upon the people of the world. *The Inverness Flyer* will deliver the proof that you are guilty of the crime of fraud, with your pathetic monster!"

"Don't talk to Lachlan like that. You're the criminal here, Fordyce. Lachlan was only trying to help the people of the village. You, on the other hand, are mean and selfish, and only think about yourself."

"That will be enough, young lady. You will respect my age."

"Oh, but I do respect your age, Major Fordyce," Mary responded sharply. "But I do not respect your actions – I do not respect what you've done. This is KIDNAPPING!"

"And you don't think that perpetrating a hoax is a crime?" said Fordyce self-righteously, then turned on his heel. Mary shook her head, sadly. She felt angry and humiliated that she had to yield like this.

Lachlan bit his lip to prevent himself from saying anything that might backfire on them, for that he would very much regret, for Mary's sake, more than anything.

The heavy cellar door banged shut, and they were left all alone, in the dark, cold dungeon.

Chapter 16

Merry Christmas to you, Laird, sir," said real estate agent Angus MacBain, as he pulled up outside the Village Hall in his lumbering Range Rover to pick up his son Gordon from the children's Christmas party. Young Gordon was well known in the village, for he had the most wondrous singing voice. He sang so beautifully that the villagers thought him to be an angel.

"Merry Christmas to you too, Angus," said Duncan as he exited the hall with Jean by his side. "You're just the man I was hoping to see today, MacBain."

"Merry Christmas to you, your ladyship," MacBain raised his hat to Jean, and gave her a generous smile.

"Young Gordon's singing brought a tear to my eye, Angus," she patted her cheek with a handkerchief as she headed off to the car.

"Does the same to me, your ladyship," MacBain nodded, as he watched her walk off.

"Yes, I'm sorry to say, Angus, that we'll be putting the castle back on the market again, and I'd like you to handle the sale for us," said Duncan.

The smile on MacBain's face faded, and his eyes moistened.

"We've made a lot of costly improvements to the castle, and I'd like you to inspect them before you start bringing prospective buyers around. Will you come and see me first thing in the New Year, Angus? We're hurrying home now, there's a blizzard forecast."

Angus's head bowed. "Aye," he said sadly. "Of course I will, your Lordship. But I'm very, very sorry to hear this. You've become very special to the villagers, Mr Campbell, Laird, sir. You and your family have become part of the place. It's a real shame. A tragedy Laird. A tragedy. Aye, it is that."

"I'm afraid that we bit off more than we could chew, Angus. You can maybe look for something smaller for us." Duncan tried hard to smile, but a smile failed to appear. Then he walked sadly to his car where Jean now waited with the children.

In his heart he deeply regretted his decision, but he knew that it was only a matter of time before the intrigue and fuss over the monster of Loch Beiste faded away, and with it, the multitude of visitors. Then the quaint little village which had become a bustling money-making metropolis, would return to its former quiet, remote self, and his debts would remain unpaid. To his mind, it was best to sell while the market was at its peak, while Airde was attracting attention around Scotland, and around the world.

#

The Campbell children sat plotting amongst themselves, huddled in a corner of the castle sitting-room beside the Christmas tree, away from grown-up ears. Robert had tried ringing Lachlan – time and time again, but there had been no answer. He had even rung Lachlan's mother, Alison MacGregor, but she hadn't seen or heard from Lachlan in days. And that wasn't like him, she said.

"Let's try the Ghillie," said Katie. "He'll know what to do."

"Good idea!" said Robert enthusiastically. He used a phone in the Great Hall, and when the phone was answered, the sounds of high-spirited revelry could be heard emanating from the Ghillie's cottage. It sounded as if a rip-roaring party was under way. Scottish Highland dance music was blaring, with yelps and whoops and screeches, followed by the thumping of feet, laughter and clapping. Robert had to shout to make himself heard when the Ghillie answered, and he had to repeat his story, countless times.

"Merry, Merry Christmas t' y', laddie." the Ghillie said jovially, then he hiccupped just like Mrs MacGivacuddle often did. "What's that y're sayin' lad? Speak up! Kidnapped? Oh aye lad, a great book that was. What's that... Mary Sinclair kidnapped? Och, now Robbie m'lad, that's the best Christmas joke ah've heard this year!" The Ghillie giggled like a little pixie. "Lachlan...? No, lad, ah have'na seen him in o'er a' week. Police? Och now, ah would'na be botherin' them the now, lad. Not at this time o'year! Besides, they're a' awa at the Lodge at the far end of Loch Beiste, catchin' salmon for a Hogmanay Feast. Get snowed-in a would'na doubt. Tee, Hee, Hee, a policeman's life for me..." he giggled.

"But Ghillie, you don't understand..." Robert was desperate to be taken seriously. He was beginning to panic about Mary. "It's Mary, she's been..."

"Bonnie lassie, that Mary. Aye, a verrrry bonnie lassie. Well now, Robbie lad, ah must awa', you've just reminded me, ah've forgotten t' wrap up the Laird's Haggis - for The New Year. A family specialty. Thanks for your 'Merry Christmas' call, Robbie, lad." And the music played on...

Robert put the phone back on its cradle and turned to Katie. "I think the Ghillie's had too much Christmas punch. He didn't understand a word I said."

The blood drained from Katie's face. "Then we'll have to call the police."

"No use. The Ghillie said Constable Brannigan and his force are all away fishing."

"But we must get some help, Robert."

"I'll ring Edinburgh," and he did. But they too were celebrating Christmas.

"A kidnapping you say, laughed the constable who answered. "Ho, Ho, Ho," he laughed, just like Father Christmas. "Now, then laddie, let's begin at the beginning, shall we? Your name please..." he requested in a deep official voice.

"But that's not important," Robert responded. "It's Mary Sinclair that's important. You've got to save her, sir, she's been kidnapped!"

"Och now, will ye hold yer horses, laddie. I canna do a thing until you give me your name and address," said the policeman gruffly. "And does your father know you're making this call? I think you'd better put him on the line. Don't you?"

Robert promptly hung up and looked round at Katie despairingly. "I knew he wouldn't listen to us kids."

"There must be someone who could help us."

"I'm going down to try and find Lachlan," said Robert, not knowing what had really happened to his friend. He was unaware that he'd been tied up in the kidnapper's truck, and now sat helpless in Fordyce's cold dungeon alongside Mary. "It's not like him at all to just disappear like this. He'll believe us! We weren't dreaming, Katie. We saw it with our own eyes."

"I'm coming too."

Just as they were reaching for their warm anoraks hanging by the kitchen door, Duncan their father came upon the scene, saying, "And where do you think you're going?"

"Out, dad," his brave son replied, trying to look cheery, and hide their real intent.

"Oh, no, you're not, young man," said his father in a very sombre tone. "I'll say this, just once, and once only, Robert Campbell, "No-one is to leave the castle tonight."

The children yelled their dismay in unison.

"But, Dad..." Their faces contorted in protesting pain.

"There will be no 'buts.' Have I made myself clear?" Duncan said resolutely. "The weather report says that a blizzard is heading this way from The Arctic Circle. It won't be safe outdoors before long."

"But Dad," Robert objected vehemently, determined to state his case. "Mary HAS been kidnapped, and Lachlan is missing. They could both be in danger."

Duncan glowered down at his son. "You just listen to me, Robert Campbell, I've had just about enough of your fanciful stories. You've got little Dottie believing this kidnapping business is true – she's quite upset about it all."

"But, Dad," Katie joined in the revolt. "It IS true!"

"That's enough from the pair of you!" Duncan snapped. "And get rid of those hang-dog looks. This is Christmas, the time to be merry. Your mother has gone to a lot of trouble to make it a happy one for you. So I don't want to hear another word tonight about Mary Sinclair, kidnapping, OR the monster. Do I make myself clear?"

Robert and Katie looked at each other. Then relented.

"Yes Dad," both sighed unhappily.

Scottie had been watching all this take place. He knew that all the odds were stacked against the children in trying to tackle this by themselves. The criminals. The storm. The danger. He knew there was a 'right' time to act, and a 'wrong' time.

"Woof" He went over to Robert, jumped up and licked his cheek as if to comfort him.

#

The blizzard had arrived. Wind began to rumble in the chimneys. It howled around the eaves like a pack of wolves. The gusts were deathly cold, and the snow drove in, in great white billows, rolling, curling, in swirling, vicious ribbons of destruction. It was the fiercest storm that the Campbells had ever experienced. They battened down all the castle windows, and pulled all the drapes.

And with blazing fires in the hearth, they felt safe inside the ancient stone structure with its six feet thick walls, and gave thought to the poor people of the world who were not so cosy and safe.

Jean sat playing the piano, sharing the piano-stool with Katie. They played Christmas carols and sang, while Robert and his father played chess. But all the while, Robert's mind was whirring, as he tried to figure out a way that he and Katie could go looking for Mary. As for Dottie, her mother had left her cuddled up to her favourite toy Koala bear, tucked up in bed fast asleep, her cheeks stained by the worried tears she had shed for Mary Sinclair.

"Checkmate!" cried Duncan, a winning smile on his face.

"Awe, Dad! Did you have to beat me on Christmas Eve?"

"I bet you wouldn't hold back from beating me!" Duncan laughed, taking a sip from his glass of Scottish whisky, a Christmas gift from Douglas Grant the publican at 'The Stag and Beiste Inn,' down in the village.

Just then, the sitting room door opened, and in traipsed little Dottie in her pyjamas.

"What are you doing out of bed, young lady?" Jean asked, holding out her arms to her dear little Dottie.

"I wok'ted up," Dottie replied, rubbing her eyes.

"Did you come all the way down that dark corridor by yourself?" Jean asked, lifting her youngest up on her knee.

"Scottie did come too," Dottie answered, tinkering with a black piano key. "And Big Man. He hold my hand."

"Oh, I see," Jean laughed. "And what did he have to say for himself?"

"Big Man said..." Dottie took a deep breath, plonked her tiny hands down on the keyboard and played a surprisingly harmonious chord. "He will finded Mary," she said matter-of-factly.

Scottie gave a resounding 'WOOF.'

"Oh, he did, did he?" Jean shared a glance and a wink with Duncan, and gave Dottie a loving hug, knowing that the tiny girl was worried about Mary.

All things considered, even with the violent storm outside, the Campbells enjoyed Christmas Eve together as a family. The children went to bed exhausted, looking forward to Christmas Day and gifts from Santa Claus, and all the many Christmas treats that would come their way. But although they were safe, and warm, and loved, their thoughts were on poor Mary, and the missing monster, as their heads touched their pillows. Where was Mary, they wondered? And what sort of Christmas Eve was she having?

Chapter 17

CHRISTMAS DAY

The family woke to find the sun. Not a timid sun. Not a meek sun. Not one that peaked gingerly through thick white clouds, but a morning sun that dazzled with brilliance in a clear blue sky. It shone on the deep blanket of snow which had fallen overnight, and made the picture-perfect village sparkle like the Milky Way.

The trees were white. The ground was white. The hills and mountains were white. Loch Beiste had a thin coating of ice. Everything as far as the eye could see was white. And it was peaceful and still, with a magic to it they had never known.

"I just know that this is going to be a terrific day, Scottie." Robert declared when Scottie woke him that morning with a lick of his tongue. "I just know it!"

Scottie woofed, and licked him on the cheek again.

"Merry Christmas, Scottie," Robert said, as he sat up in bed and gave his best friend a big hug. To which, Scottie responded the way that dogs do. With more licks, and nuzzles, and funny little noises as if they're trying to talk.

Robert bounded out of bed. "I have a gift for you, Scottie," and he scampered over to the fireplace in his bedroom – every room in the castle had a huge stone fireplace, with not necessarily a fire in it – and he reached for a small red stocking hanging there that Katie had made for their canine friend, then hurried back to put his feet under the bedclothes again. With a broad grin, Robert presented Scottie with his very own Christmas stocking. "There you go, Scottie."

Scottie's long nose foraged inside the stocking, and, with tail wagging, he latched onto something down at the bottom. But when he tried to extract it, the stocking stayed jammed over his nose, and he couldn't dislodge it. At first he tried to pull it off with a paw. Then, in an effort to free himself, he pranced around the room with his snout still inside the red stocking, shaking his head and growling at the stocking.

Robert thought it was the funniest sight he had ever seen. He laughed and laughed at his funny friend, and this only made Scottie start barking a muffled bark from inside the stocking, as if to say, 'Come on, Robert, help me get this off.'

All this noise brought the two girls into Robert's room. Both were dressed in their thick tartan dressing-gowns and woolly slippers. They each carried a red stocking Katie had made.

"What's going on?" queried Katie.

Robert didn't have to explain.

"Wook at Scottie."

"Come on, Scottie, I'll help you," said Robert patting the bed. Scottie jumped up beside him, tail wagging.

When Robert pulled the red stocking off Scottie's nose, they saw that Scottie had a tight grip of the gift in his mouth – a brand new collar. A red tartan collar, with the words 'Scottie The Wonder Dog – Castle Airde' professionally burnt into the leather by the village blacksmith.

They all agreed it was the finest collar in the village, and Robert fastened it around Scottie's neck with love.

"Woof, Woof," came his thanks.

Then the girls presented Robert with a gift. Katie had knitted Robert a long red scarf.

"Thanks, Katie." Then Dottie presented her gift to her big brother. "What's this, Dottie?" he asked, unfurling a paper scroll his little sister had handed him. "A picture that you painted?"

"That Big Man," she said proudly. Her 'Big Man' was wearing a breast-plate of armour, he carried a shield, and wore a Scottish kilt, and had long hair.

"Thanks, Dottie, he looks like a nice Big Man." He gave her a hug.

"Yeth," she said, thrusting her thumb into her mouth with a shy glance to Katie.

Robert looked at the painting long, and hard. It was just a simple sketch, from a mite not yet three years old, but he sensed there was something special about it. "I'll ask Lachlan to make a frame for it, and I'll keep it here, above my bed."

Each looked at the other at the mention of Lachlan's name.

"I wonder what's happened to Mary," said Katie, suddenly sad again.

"We've got to find her. And Lachlan, too," Robert declared, looking out the window. "The blizzard's stopped now. We'll start looking for them after breakfast."

Scottie barked his agreement.

"After we get pwesents," said Dottie.

"Yes, Dottie," said the older children, smiling, "After we get lots of pwesents," and they headed downstairs for breakfast.

#

Breakfast time was a happy time. There was delightful expectancy in the air, for the Christmas presents sat waiting at the foot of the tree, while a fire blazed in the kitchen hearth.

"We'll be able to build a snowman, Robert," said Katie, spreading another hot pancake with Kieller's Highland Heather Honey.

"Yes, after we've found the two 'M's, he whispered.

'What two 'M's?'

"Mary and the monster, you dummy," he hissed quietly.

"Oh!" Katie nodded.

"A snowman, what a good idea," said Jean with a wink to Duncan. "Well now, perhaps there are Christmas presents waiting to be opened that might suit this weather. Who knows? I'm sure Santa is a practical man as well as a generous one. Don't you agree, Duncan?"

"Oh, I'm sure he is, my dear."

"I see that Scottie already has his gift, said Jean, "and doesn't it suit him." Scottie bounded over for a hug from Jean at the mention of his name. "Well now, as soon as everyone's finished breakfast, we'll see if Santa's been good to us, too."

"Pwesents!" Dottie excitedly called out.

"Can we go out after breakfast?" Robert asked, thinking about the two 'M's and Lachlan.

"What for?" Duncan scowled. He was surprised that Robert was showing such little interest in Christmas gifts, and was about to ask why, when he was interrupted by the telephone which began to ring insistently. "Hold everything," said Duncan, as he moved to answer the phone.

And when he did, and heard the voice of Major Fordyce, his face suddenly lost its glow of 'goodwill.' "You do realise that its Christmas Morning, Major?" This was followed by a short pause. "Oh, very well!" Duncan said in a most disenchanted tone, thrusting down the telephone with a clatter. He turned to his family, and said, "Get dressed everybody. There's an urgent village meeting in half an hour. The presents will have to wait." The look of disapproval on Jean's face made him speak out again, adding a waggle of his forefinger. "And don't you say a word, Jean Campbell. I am The Laird of Airde, remember. And duty calls!"

#

Although much snow had fallen overnight, the castle was not snowed-in. The Campbells managed to make it down to the bottom of the hill in Jean's Australian station-wagon, but the winding journey was taken with the greatest of care, with snow chains on the wheels. It was the quietest car journey Duncan could ever remember. The children all held their breath as the car emerged from the tunnel at a slippery snail's pace, to tackle the snow-covered, narrow winding road. The knuckles beneath their gloves were white as they gripped tight to the back of the front seat.

When they reached the end of the steep decline, the whole family breathed a great sigh of relief. Then, Duncan nosed the car out into the T-Junction, and was about to take the road left to the village, when suddenly, Scottie began to bark. And he barked and barked, non-stop. This puzzled the Campbells. They could see nothing unusual anywhere around.

"What's got you all worked up, Scottie?" asked Duncan.

Then suddenly a huge black truck zoomed past, sending snow and slush flying, headed for the village.

"That's the baddies truck!" Kate exclaimed.

"That's the truck we were telling you about, Dad," Robert yelled. "Scottie must have known." He smiled at Scottie and patted him.

Scottie stopped barking, and without any help whatsoever from anyone, opened the car door by pulling up the lock with his teeth and pushing down the handle with a paw. Before anyone could stop him, he jumped out into the freezing white snow, and took off down the road – to the right – not the left toward the village.

"Where's he off to?" Duncan queried.

"Follow him, Dad. He's trying to tell us something."

"Damn it, Robert, I have a meeting to attend." Duncan snapped back sharply.

"But Dad, it must be really important. Scottie's never done anything like this before, ever!"

"That's right, Dad," agreed Katie.

"Scottie is cwever dog. Never bark like this time," added Dottie, shaking her head from side to side.

"We can spare a moment or two Duncan," Jean dared. "The meeting can't possibly start without you. You are the Laird, after all." She smiled sweetly at her husband. She knew that her best smile usually did the trick of swaying him, one way or the other.

"Oh, alright. Alright!" Then Duncan turned the wheel to the right toward Fordyce's property, instead of going down toward the village.

Scottie was well ahead of them by the time the decision was made. At first, he had barked and barked to show the way, then, when he knew that they were following, he bounded off as fast as the wind. His long, pointed nose leading the way, and his thick bushy tail flying out behind.

Approaching Major Fordyce's wrought-iron gate, which had been left wide open, he stopped, and panting, turned to check that the Campbell's car was not far behind. He gave out a loud "Woof" as the Campbell's station wagon slid to a halt, waiting to see what he was up to. Then, he turned and sped along the Major's driveway knowing that they would follow.

"He wants us to go in there?" queried Duncan. "Into Fordyce's property?"

"Yeees!" said the children in unison. "Hurry!"

Jean looked across at her husband with a 'Well, what are you waiting for?' look on her face, and nodded her encouragement.

"Okay," he said, uncertainly. "But I have no idea what this is leading to."

Neither Fordyce nor his Land Rover, was anywhere to be seen, as the Campbells traversed the bumpy laneway toward

Fordyce's grey stone house, to see Scottie waiting for them at the door to the barn.

Duncan pulled up, and they all disembarked to head toward where Scottie was digging at the bottom of the barn door.

"Come on." Robert called out impatiently to the others, as he was first to arrive at the scene, and he started to push at the great fifteen-foot high wooden door which let out deep groans from infrequent use. It proved to be way too difficult to open. He would definitely need his father to help him.

But Scottie was able to thrust his nose in between the two halves of the door, and pushed past Robert into the vast space. Duncan, with Robert's help eventually pushed the mighty old doors open, and in they all went. Again Scottie began to bark, for the light now suddenly shone on Magnus guarding the trap door, and the ugly hound was growling, and showing his teeth ready to do battle.

But Scottie was not afraid of the British Bulldog. He crouched down like a sheep dog, moving stealthily toward the ugly animal, he barked at the unsightly, overweight hound, showing that he was ready to go on the attack, but instead, he took off, out of the barn, with Magnus chasing after him, his slobbering jaws dripping with saliva. Scottie was the much fitter and faster of the two canines, and led Magnus on a merry dance down the lane, until the fat hound was forced to come to a panting halt, and collapsed in a panting heap, unable to take another step. Still panting.

Now, with the light beaming in through the open barn door, Robert was able to spot the trap door in the floor, where Magnus had stood guard. He pointed it out to his parents, so they hastened toward it. It took all of Duncan's strength to heave and pull it up and open.

"Hello... anybody there?" He called out as his family watched on.

"Help!" Came the sweet sound of Mary Sinclair's voice.

"We're down here," yelled Lachlan. "They tied us up."

Duncan and Jean looked at each other in absolute amazement. "How on earth did Scottie know they were down here?"

Robert wasted no time in hurrying down the wooden steps into the freezing cold dungeon beneath the barn, to find Lachlan and Mary tied to a timber beam.

"Well done, lad," Lachlan said, smiling for the first time in many hours.

"Thank Heaven you found us, Robert," Mary said gratefully, giving her rescuers a grand smile, as Duncan joined his son in climbing down to untie the pair.

"How DID you find us, Robert, my boy?"

"Scottie brought us," Robert said proudly, untying Mary.

"Oh, thank you, Robert," said Mary, rubbing her sore wrists. "Thank you for rescuing us." She wrapped her arms around Robert and gave him a big bear hug, making Robert blush.

After stretching their sore, stiff limbs to get the circulation of blood flowing, they climbed up the stairs, and left the dungeon behind. Jean took off her coat and wrapped it around a shivering, and very grateful, Mary Sinclair, knowing that there were tartan rugs in the car.

"Thank you, so much, Mrs Campbell," said Mary. "I'm fine now, just a wee bit sore, and a wee bit cold, but we'll live."

"Well," said Duncan. "It's taught me something! Next time my children insist on telling me a 'story', no matter how fanciful it sounds, I'll not only listen, but I'll act on it. I'm ashamed of myself, I didn't believe a word you children were telling me. It won't happen again. I'm truly sorry!"

"That's okay, Dad," said Robert. "I know it was a lot to believe. Now what are you going to do about the Major?"

"He naughty man," commented Dottie, taking her thumb out of her mouth to make her declaration.

"Come on, everyone, we have a meeting to go to." And he ushered the two rescued captives out and into the car.

"Aye," Lachlan agreed. "We've got to put a stop to Major Fordyce's little game."

Scottie, standing guard by the car let out a great 'Woof'.

Chapter 18

Marching boldly toward the gathered crowd, then pushing his way through, as if his very life depended on reaching the far side, Major Fordyce, with Marjory Meddle hurrying along behind him, climbed up onto his soapbox at MacTaggart's Landing; that long stone jetty that jutted out into the beautiful Loch Beiste - where he could be seen from every angle - and prepared to make an earth-shattering announcement, megaphone in hand.

Everyone in the village had been alerted. All had gathered at the Village Green. From the oldest resident, one hundred and twenty year old Tobias Robert Bruce, the shoemaker, to the very tiniest, Louise Dundee McGhee, born on St Andrews day only weeks before, who lay wrapped in a cosy bundle in her mother's arms.

Not a soul, not a mite had stayed away. Every living person from the village, and hordes of journalists from newspapers, radio-station disk-jockeys, who gabbled non-stop into microphones, and television crews with their multitude of cameras and equipment, had come from all around the world expecting an exciting, scientific announcement about the monster of Loch Beiste.

Standing atop his soapbox, the Major surveyed the scene, casting his eyes over the sea of faces. He craned his neck, he pried, he spied, he squinted, he peered from his vantage point, inspecting every head, and every hat, to locate the Laird. But the Laird was nowhere to be seen.

Then, he cleared his throat, lifted the megaphone to his lips, and with every eye upon him, he began his bombast, while

Marjory Meddle, standing proudly at his side, smirked like a contented Cheshire Cat.

"Ladies, gentlemen, and children of Airde," the supercilious Fordyce boomed, "we have waited long enough for The Laird of Airde to make his appearance here today. Sadly, it seems, he has more important, er, personal things he chooses to do, than preside over this most auspicious gathering." His gaze scanned the sea of upturned faces, with a sneer upon his own. "Therefore," he continued, in his customary pompous fashion, "it is my solemn duty to convey to you this fine Christmas morning, that a dastardly double-cross has been perpetrated against the people of Airde, and on the world!"

There was an audible gasp of shock from the gathered crowd.

"It is true, my fellow Airdians. A ghastly crime has been committed, and you, you, have been made to look foolish in the eyes of the world."

There was another gasp from the crowd.

"We'll be needin' proof of yer accusation, Fordyce," the Ghillie called out sceptically.

"All in good time, my man," was the Major's snide reply, as he thumped down his walking stick over and over again, to gain back his audience's undivided attention, before he resumed his tirade. "It is a fact that you, naïve simpletons - have been hood-winked! Yes, you have been hood-winked... you are nothing but gullible, foolish bogons."

There was an angry mumble from the crowd, for the villagers were becoming increasingly irritated by his criticism. Pride was important to the Airdians.

"What is it that you're saying, Major Fordyce?" queried Reverend Brown.

"Aye. Out with it, man!" the Ghillie concurred, pushing his way to the front of the crowd.

116

"I am about to unveil the truth to you," Fordyce snarled. "Let me tell you, that it is The Laird of Airde and his family who have conspired against you, along with that mischief-maker, Lachlan MacGregor and his cohort, Mary Sinclair. They are the ones to blame."

The crowd was shocked to hear this.

"Bring on the truck," yelled Fordyce through his loudspeaker. "Bring on the truck!"

The engine of the big black truck roared into life from nearby. The crowd moved uncertainly to one side, as the clumsy vehicle slowly reversed to halt nearby Fordyce. Then three burly strangers clambered down from the truck's cabin – Boris, Thumper, and Dingbat. They stood at the rear of the vehicle and waited for a command from their employer.

"Ladies, gentlemen and children of Airde," Fordyce began gloatingly, "permit me to be the one to reveal this most hideous of crimes against you." He turned again to his helpers. "Drop the tailgate, gentlemen," he ordered with a dramatic sweep of his gun-head walking stick.

The three men flicked up the flap of the rear tarpaulin, dropped the tail gate, and then clambered up into the truck.

Very soon, there were noises of metal scraping against metal emanating from inside the truck. There was a clang and a bang, a smack and a whack, a plunk, and a plonk, a click and a clack, a crash and a smash from inside. Till suddenly, huge chunks of metal came hurtling dangerously from the truck, to fall to the ground. And very soon, there was a pile of black metal scattered before the eyes of the people of Airde. Metal, with what looked like old bath mats attached to it.

"This, you gullible people, is your Loch Beiste Beast!"

A profound, lung-filling gasp emanated from every witness. And each one turned to another in disbelief, eyes wide with shocked surprise.

"Now you see what a fraudulent hoax has been perpetrated by The Laird and his cohorts. Now you see how the world will laugh at Airde. I tell you now, that the Campbells are behind this scurrilous imitation monster of the lake. They devised it, Lachlan MacGregor created it, and Mary Sinclair publicised it! Just so those dastardly, cheating, criminal Australians could attract tourists to their castle."

As one, every head in the crowd looked down to their toes in embarrassment.

But just then, a car horn was heard blasting out across the valley. It went on and on, getting closer and closer to the gathered crowd, until the now, very much saddened people of Airde, turned around to look in its direction, to see what the fuss was about.

Speeding down William Wallace Drive towards them was Jean Campbell's station wagon, its horn blasting non-stop. It was soon upon the scene. The crowd parted, as the vehicle slowly, and carefully, made its way through the throng, to stop near the front of the gathering. The Laird of Airde had arrived!

"Stop this charade!" cried Duncan Campbell from the driver's seat, his head thrust out of the window, his fist thrust defiantly in the air. The proud and dutiful Laird of Airde opened his driver's side door, got out, and marched boldly through the gawking crowd to stand in front of his accuser. "Before you start pointing fingers, and condemning people, Major Fordyce, let the good people decide who the really guilty party is here!"

The crowd was astonished. So much was happening, so very fast. Now too, they saw the rest of the Campbells, together with Lachlan MacGregor and Mary Sinclair emerging from the car. All the players in the drama had now assembled.

"Too late, Campbell, your scheme has been exposed," Fordyce smugly declared.

"Is that so?" Duncan stood with arms folded, glaring at Fordyce as they stood toe to toe, while the village bore witness to the scene. "You and your partner in crime, Marjory Meddle, along with these three out-of-town villains are guilty of KIDNAPPING!"

The crowd let out its loudest gasp yet, while cameras flashed and clicked, and reporter's microphones were thrust under Duncan's nose.

"It's true." Mary Sinclair called out, as she and the others gathered around Duncan.

"Yes. KIDNAPPING!" Duncan repeated. Scottie had run to stand by Duncan's side, and let out a resounding 'Woof' every time the word KIDNAPPING was uttered. "The beautiful young Mary Sinclair, and brave Lachlan MacGregor here, were held against their will by these hooligans, and left to freeze in the cellar beneath Fordyce's barn last night, in below zero temperatures, and we can all remember how cold it was last night."

There were mumbles of agreement from the crowd.

"It's a lie!" Fordyce exclaimed, his voice trembling just a little.

"Lachlan and I will both testify at your trial, Major Fordyce," Mary declared with satisfaction. "It took three of your brutes to capture Lachlan, you know. If it hadn't been for him keeping my spirits up, I might not have made it through the long, cold night."

"Aye," Lachlan agreed, "a sweet little thing like Mary shouldn't be treated like that."

"It's a lie, I tell you," Fordyce persisted. "It's their word against mine."

"We saw it too," young Robert chimed in. "We saw the truckies capture Mary, and we saw them both trust up in the Major's cold barn. With Magnus the brute, standing guard."

"Yes, we did," Katie joined in. "And Mrs Meddle was there too. I saw her!"

A loud gasp of incredulity emitted from every mouth.

Marjory Meddle, the Major's female accomplice went pale, and clutched her bosom at the mention of her name. "Oooooh!"

"Hobble men," said Dottie, holding onto her mother's coattails.

As the family stood, huddled together in a group with Lachlan and Mary in front of the stunned crowd, and the media people jostling for the best positions, shouting a barrage of questions at them, Constable Brannigan who had only that morning returned from his fishing trip, stepped forward in his customary custodian role.

"I take it, Lachlan," the policeman began, with chest much puffed inside his uniform, "that The Laird has his facts straight, m'lad?"

"Aye, he does, Constable Brannigan. That mean-spirited Fordyce did take this lovely young lass and myself hostage, and while the people of the village were all safe and snug in their own warm beds last night, this poor wee lass was left to shiver in Fordyce's cellar all through that terrible storm."

Constable Brannigan looked deeply into Mary Sinclair's eyes, and saw the truth in them. He knew that such pretty blue eyes could never lie.

Then a lone voice cried out from the crowd. "Shame on you, Fordyce." It was the Reverend Brown. "Shame!"

"Aye, shame on you," the Ghillie agreed. "The man should be hung, drawn and quartered, just like they did to our great patriot, William Wallace."

The whole crowd cried out in agreement. "SHAME!"

Thrusting out his chest even further, in true constable fashion, Brannigan went into action. "You two wicked folk," he decreed, to Fordyce and Meddle, "can come wi' me then, an spend your Christmas Day in lock-up. See how ye like that!"

And with a mighty swoop, he pulled Fordyce down off his soapbox, and grabbed him by the scruff of the neck, took the protesting Marjory Meddle by the arm, and led the nasty pair away, while the Ghillie, and some other men of the village collared the three truckies.

The crowd started a slow-clap, simultaneously shouting, "SHAME, SHAME, SHAME," as all the kidnappers were marched away to the village's tiny police station.

No-one had noticed that Scottie had scampered off. No-one had noticed that he'd sat himself down at the far end of the stone jetty, where the water was deeper, to look out over Loch Beiste. He sat there waiting, and watching, till a delicate shadow of mist which had hovered over the lake throughout proceedings began to disperse. Then he began to bark, one of his attention-seeking barks, to alert the people of Airde to what was about to happen.

Everyone turned to look in his direction, and Robert came running down the jetty to see what he was up to. "What is it, Scottie, what is it, boy?"

Scottie jumped up and licked Robert's cheek, than sat back down again, gazing out into the silver water. Robert's eyes scanned the shimmering lake and its far horizon, to see if he could see what it was that had taken Scottie's attention. But there was nothing to be seen, except melting patches of thin ice floating gently on the beautiful lake.

Everything, all around, was suddenly eerily still, and silent. But amidst that stillness, amidst that quiet, a distant, haunting skirl of bagpipes could be heard wrapping the scene in a cloak of Scottish magic.

What was about to happen would change the life of the people of Airde for evermore! For, not far from the shore, the water of the lake suddenly erupted in a gigantic pool of frothy bubbles, and a sleek, black, serpent-like head emerged, and cut through the water with a series of humps following along behind. The watching villagers gasped as they had never gasped before.

A great geyser of water spurted into the air as the creature bobbed and ducked and splashed in the lake like a nubile mermaid, displaying itself proudly for the benefit of the crowd.

The villagers could not believe their eyes. It took the astute Mary Sinclair to point out the obvious truth to them all.

"If this here, on the ground, is the fake monster," she said, pointing to the pile of crumpled metal, "then that must be the REAL monster of Lake Beiste!"

Major Fordyce promptly fainted in the arms of Constable Brannigan, while Marjory Meddle anxiously tried to revive him by waving her hat over him like a fan.

Meanwhile, Mary, grinning, grabbed Lachlan's arm, and when little Dottie reached out her arms to her, she swooped her up. Then, Mary grabbed hold of Katie's hand, and ran with them towards Robert and Scottie, to stand down at the far end of MacTaggart's Landing to get a better view. Duncan and Jean chased after them, with all the media people taking up their cameras to capture the real monster on film, while the crowd 'oohed' and 'aahed' in wonder.

"A real monster of the lake, Scottie," said Robert in wonderment, to his beloved friend Scottie, giving him a cuddle. His little heart bursting inside his chest with glee.

Others from the village ran excitedly onto the jetty to watch in amazement, the sight of their very own, and very real, Loch Beiste Monster, in spellbound silence, as it ducked and dived, cavorting playfully on the lake.

It was Dottie who first noticed the something extra – and she shouted for everyone to hear. "The Lady of The Lake has a little baby!" And sure enough, gliding gracefully through the silver pond was a protective mother, proudly showing off her new born baby.

"What a day. What a sight. What a Christmas. What a Blessing! The villagers had their pride restored, and would now be

122

able to enjoy the wondrous sight of their very own 'Beiste' in their very own lake – Lake Beiste. There was joy in every Airdian heart.

Chapter 19

The remainder of Christmas Day was a happy one for the villagers; they had much to celebrate. It was especially so for the Campbells who had yet to open their Christmas presents.

Santa had indeed been good to the children. Katie was presented with a pair of ice-skates, as well as the many books she'd wished for. Robert was pleased to find a camera in one of his parcels, but thrilled to find fantastic computer games in his stocking. Dottie was given a three-wheeled bicycle to get her around the castle quicker than before, and the most beautiful doll that one could ever wish to see, dressed as a Scottish Highland dancer.

The Campbells had invited Lachlan and Mary back to share their joy at the castle, but the brave, tired pair, had each said they would return to their own homes, to make it a happy day for their own mothers, who had worried about them. But not before they had said their grateful thanks to their rescuers.

"I'm in your debt, Robert Campbell," Lachlan began. "I'd like to show you how grateful I am. How would you like me to make you a really smart looking snow sledge?"

"Oh, wow!" he said, turning to Scottie. "We'd have some fun with that, wouldn't we Scottie?"

"Woof!" was Scottie's reply, and he jumped up and placed his paws on Lachlan's big strong chest, and licked his cheek to show his appreciation.

"You could help me work on it Robert, if you wanted to. Make it to your own design."

"That would be great, Lachlan," said Robert excitedly. "Once I learned how to do that, I could make all sorts of gadgets for my room. Oh, and some handy things for Mum, and Dad, too," he added quickly.

"And what about you two young ladies?" Lachlan asked, smiling down at Dottie, "I fancy that a doll's house wouldn't go astray now, would it?"

Katie looked quickly down at Dottie to see her reaction.

"Dolls houth," she said, jumping up and down. "Big, like castle," she smiled, arms outstretched. "With chairs and tables, and beds, and dolls, and..."

Lachlan laughed. "All right, lass. All right. I'll see what I can do," he winked at Mary standing by his side. "But in the meantime. I'll be taking Mary home, she's been through quite an ordeal this last couple of days. Come on, lass, you'll be needing a good rest after all this excitement."

"Nonsense, Lachlan. I've got a story to write. My photographer got all the action on his video camera. I'm going to write a documentary for Scottish television. It could win me the John Logie Baird Trophy," she smiled.

#

The next few days went very quickly. Soon it would be New Year's Eve, and down at Major Fordyce's front gate, a loud tap, tap, tapping, could be heard. It was Angus MacBain the Real Estate agent who was banging a 'For Sale' sign into the ground, in front of the Major's farm. Neither Major Fordyce nor Marjory Meddle wanted to show their face in the village of Airde ever again, for they were not welcome there.

Constable Brannigan had suggested to them, that if they left the district, he would let them go free. So, that very same day, the

Reverend Brown married the pair, in jail, then they hurried home and made arrangements to flee away to another place - in disgrace!

They chose John O'Groats as their new abode, which sits on the northernmost tip of Scotland.

A quiet place, except for the annual marathon to Lands' End, which attracts a multitude of tourists, and the John O'Groats Bake-Off, which attracts the world's best chefs, the Arctic Expeditions, bringing world scientists. The Submarine Stations' noisy war games, the fishing industry's 'Catch A Wriggly Salmon' competition, the knitting and weaving industry's 'Make a Bonnie Bonnet,' the hard-working, merry-making, oil riggers on shore-leave, and the heart-rending bleating, from near frozen sheep, bred for their tough carpet wool. The 'Catcha Porky Pig Competition,' and the Whisky Festival's 'Drink A Dram.' And all the many conventions held there, where thousands of people congregated from all around the world. John O'Groats was infamous for its lively activity – all year round. And of course, it's an icy-cold, and stormy place. Constable Brannigan knew all this, but intentionally forgot to warn the newly-weds, but wished them every happiness, none-the-less.

A day or so after Angus MacBain had put the 'For Sale' sign up at the Major's farm, and another at Marjory Meddle's cottage in the village, he came calling on Duncan Campbell at the castle, as promised.

"Hello there, Mr Campbell, Laird, sir," said the amiable man, holding out his hand when greeted by Duncan at the castle door. "Before Christmas, Mr Campbell, sir, you asked me to call and see you about selling the castle," he said, sadly.

"Welcome, Angus, welcome. Come in, come in," said Duncan cheerily.

"Thank you, Laird, sir, but I won't be stopping. I just came to tell you that I've found a rich, Arabian oil man who wants to buy the castle, sight unseen. I just want your permission to make the necessary arrangements."

"But that won't be necessary, Angus," Duncan advised, looking into Angus's puzzled face. "You see, we won't be selling the castle now after all. We're very happy here, and the Loch Beiste Monster is providing us with a steady stream of paying house guests. I've also just received word from the U.S.A. that I've won a big computer contract. So, it looks like our future here in Airde is secure." Then he grinned, with a twinkle in his eye. "I might even buy a new Jaguar, Angus." He added a wink.

Angus's face lit up. He held out his hand to Duncan and shook it heartily. "I'm so very glad to her that, Laird, sir. So very glad indeed!" he responded happily. "It's a great, great way to start the new year!" And off he went, muttering happily to himself.

#

It was the night of the Grand Hogmanay Ball. In Scotland, 'Hogmanay' – the night before the first day of the New Year, is the biggest occasion of the whole year. And here it was! This was the night that Mary Sinclair, had promised Lachlan MacGregor, that she would save the last dance just for him! A night, when The Laird would wear his full regal regalia, and Jean would wear her best red velvet gown, with a white silk sash draped across the bodice and over her left shoulder, fixed with a Cairngorm thistle brooch. The Campbell children would also attend. Children were always included at events such as these, for in Scotland, little fun could be had without young children.

In the gaily decorated Village Hall, kilts swirled to the bagpipes as they played a merry tune, and the happy people danced throughout the night to welcome in The New Year. When it came time for the very last dance, Lachlan, dressed in the rich burgundy hunting tartan of the MacGregor's, made his way boldly over to the lovely Mary Sinclair, to ask her for the honour of dancing the last dance with her.

"You look very, very beautiful tonight, Mary," said Lachlan looking into Mary's dazzling blue eyes, as he held her tiny waist, and twirled her around the dance-floor with all eyes of the crowd upon them.

"You're looking mighty braw yourself, tonight, Lachlan," she replied.

"I'm a happy man, Mary." He continued with a jaunty air. "For here I am, dancing with the prettiest girl in the room, with the hope of a wee kiss at the stroke of midnight to bring in the New Year."

Mary smiled a coy smile at the thought of kissing Lachlan. "You're very sure of yourself, Lachlan," she said, as the room seemed to spin around her as they danced.

"Well now, Mary. You know that I'm a descendent of the famous, Rob Roy, don't you? It's he that must take the credit for my pluck."

"A wee kiss on Hogmanay won't worry a daring lass like me, Lachlan MacGregor! My ancestors were brave fighting men, too, you know. Sir William St Clair accompanied The Black Douglas back to Scotland with the heart of Robert The Bruce, after the big battle in Spain."

"Is that so, Mary...?" Lachlan asked cheekily. Then he began to sprout about his famous ancestors, never wanting to be outdone, especially by just a sweet young lass like Mary. "Well I'll have you know," he countered, "that my great, great, great, grandfather..."

"Was an outlaw!" laughed Mary, and the two young people continued on like this, joking and competing, like playful puppies, until two minutes before midnight, at which time, Lachlan took Mary's hand, and led her outside, on to the doorstep, where they could be alone.

The scene before them was quiet and still. The wild merriment behind them, inside, behind the closed door of the hall. Feeling as if they were the only two people in the whole world, they stood looking out across the magnificent, still, white landscape, as the stars of the Milky Way twinkled from a clear, pitch black sky, and the moon shone down on the silky smooth snow, and shimmered on the glass-like lake. With their breath steaming on the chill night air, hand in hand they stood enjoying the moment, as the church bells began their chime to greet in the New Year. And on the stroke of Midnight, Duncan turned to Mary, looked deep into her dewy eyes and kissed her.

#

It was close to one o'clock in the morning when the Campbells arrived home from the Hogmanay Ball, tired, but happy. It was the only night of the year the youngsters were allowed to stay up so late. They happily readied for bed, after hugs and kisses from their parents.

"It's been a wonderful night, Duncan," said Jean to her husband, as they sat side by side on the sofa in their sitting room, holding hands. I'm glad that everything has turned out so well. I feel so blessed that we're able to keep the castle. You know, this is the happiest we've ever been, you and I. The children love it here too."

Duncan nodded. "What I'm glad about Jean, is that everything has worked out so well for the village. It's had its pride restored, and it will prosper now – thanks to The Lady of the Lake." He squeezed her hand affectionately, and smiled at his precious wife.

"Yes, thanks to The Lady. What a miracle she turned out to be." The contented couple lingered in front of the still burning embers of the fire in the hearth, thinking over the events of the past few weeks, when everything had at first seemed so bleak, but was now so rosy. And they shared a look of love as they sat together in peaceful reverie.

Upstairs, in pyjamas, with teeth clean and warm beds waiting, Robert shouted out, "Anyone seen Scottie? He's not at the bottom of my bed tonight."

The girls came into Robert's bedroom to check for themselves.

"Katie stood shaking her head with a worried look on her face, but Dottie smiled, knowingly.

"I see him, I see." And just when Robert was about to ask where Dottie had seen him, they heard his distant bark.

"Where's that coming from?"

"Scottie out there, Wobert," Dottie said, pointing to his window. "Dottie see him."

"Outside?" Robert said incredulously. "In the cold?"

"Big Man with Scottie," Dottie said.

"Woof!" Came Scottie's bark from below their window.

The three Campbell children scampered over to peer out of Robert's window. Below, in the open courtyard, a thick mist hovered, then began swirling round and round in a circular motion.

Scottie continued to bark. Then, as the children watched, the mist began to clear a little, and soon, they were able to see him sitting in the snow, looking up at their bedroom window. Beside him, stood a giant of a man. A man at least seven feet tall. A magnificent-looking warrior, clad in ancient tartan, carrying a heavy shield, and wearing a mighty sword.

The mystical figure smiled warmly at the children, then gave them a respectful bow.

"See... Big Man!" said Dottie excitedly.

"That's William Wallace – The Guardian of Scotland," said Robert in amazement. "Just like the painting in the library."

"The man from hundreds of years ago?" asked Katie in disbelief.

Robert nodded, unable to take his eyes off the giant in the snow. "He's Scotland's greatest hero. And that's the man in the picture you drew for me, Dottie," he exclaimed. "But...but...how can it possibly be...?"

"Big Man," Dottie repeated proudly. "My Big Man."

The ancient warrior, The Guardian of Scotland, from 700 years before, turned, and with knightly bearing, began to walk slowly toward the six-foot thick, stone castle wall. Then, to the utter amazement of the watching children, he melted into the wall, and was gone. And trotting by his side went Scottie, disappearing before their eyes, like his Master of old.

THE END